Contents

Chapter One 3
Chapter Two 17
Chapter Three 23
Chapter Four 29
Chapter Five 44
Chapter Six 51
Chapter Seven 55
Chapter Eight 70
Chapter Nine 77
Chapter Ten 87
Chapter Eleven 94
Chapter Twelve 98
Chapter Thirteen 105
Chapter Fourteen 116
Chapter Fifteen 122
Chapter Sixteen 128
Chapter Seventeen 133
Chapter Eighteen 139
Chapter Nineteen 141
Chapter Twenty 147
Chapter Twenty-One 158
Acknowledgements 165
Q&A 166

A Christmas Coral (Chapter One) 169

Chapter One

Corbin had always clung to the belief that death would eventually release him from the weight of human interaction.

However, to his dismay, he instead found himself at the centre of a lively television studio, surrounded by thousands of enthusiastic audience members.

Many of these spectators were pointing, laughing, and taunting.

Whilst feeling exposed and vulnerable like never before, Corbin struggled to comprehend how he had ended up here in such a bizarre situation.

A sudden sharp stinging sensation at the side of his neck made him wince. He gently touched a new scar, once again unsure of how it had come to be there.

The intensity of the studio lights cast a stark spotlight on the man; a silver-haired handsome aristocrat in the prime of his early-fifties, with his look of bewilderment on full display for all to see.

Three hefty cameras were positioned in place right before a confident voice boomed out through the speakers, "Welcome to another gripping episode of 'This *Was* Your Life'."

As the audience erupted into thunderous applause, a stunning woman waltzed onto the stage with a microphone in one hand and a large red leather-bound book in the other. Written on the cover in big bold letters was the title of the show.

This host embodied the typical glamour often expected of someone in her public-facing role, with an hourglass figure, impeccably applied makeup, and red hair that swayed with each step. However, an unusual sight marred her appearance. She too had a mark on her neck. Handprint bruises seemed to bear witness to a recent violent attack. Unfazed by the painful-looking injury, she locked her gaze on a camera and declared, "I'm Karina Reed, and today, we delve into the colourful life and enigmatic demise of Mr. Corbin Armstrong. Towards the end of his life, he stood as the wealthiest man on Earth, frequently hailed by the media and his peers as the most brilliant tech visionary of our time. *Never* before have we welcomed a guest as *captivating* as the one before me."

Wanting no part in this, the perplexed man bolted toward the illuminated emergency exit sign, desperate to make his escape. He barely took a few steps before the show's formidable security guard, Bones, seized him with a powerful grip, effortlessly steering the reluctant star back to his seat.

The remaining crew members consisted of a lively mix of both humans and well-trained feral beasts. The creatures took charge of various essential roles, such as operating the cameras, managing the lighting, overseeing the control room, and even ensuring that everyone's appetites were satisfied through their surprisingly exceptional catering skills. They also proved to be adept salespeople, using their persuasive pitch: "Advertise with us, or we'll eat you."

During commercial breaks, Cuddles, the seasoned entertainer, would emerge from the wings, ready to engage the audience with some stand-up comedy and maintain their enthusiasm. And finally, overseeing this entire operation was Be-Be, serving as both the Producer and Director, skilfully orchestrating the show with precision and style.

Be-Be had eagerly awaited this very interview for the longest time. The lifestyle chosen by Corbin revolted her, branding him as the ultimate embodiment of moral decay. As she observed with keen anticipation, waiting to see how he would attempt to justify his actions, her focus was suddenly drawn to an unexpected development. While the show's star was under the intense scrutiny of most audience members, one random elderly woman instead directed her unwavering stare toward Be-Be, sending a shiver down her spine. What troubled the Producer even more was that, for the first time in decades, the skilled master of manipulation found herself unable to penetrate someone's mind. It was as if Be-Be were peering into nothing more than an empty void. She ultimately brushed off the situation, attributing it to the possibility of her exhaustion, which stemmed from the demands of ruling Hell.

Diverting her attention back to the show, Be-Be instructed the camera operators to, "Zoom in on Corbin. I want to see the sweat beads on his brow as this story of his unfolds." She then added, "Over to you, Miss Reed. Do your thing. Make him suffer."

The presenter proceeded to ask her guest, "Do you know what's happening right now?"

With a visibly racing heart, the star of the show responded, "I... I'm dead, aren't I?"

"We prefer the term 'Life Challenged', but yes."

"And if I were to hazard a guess... as crazy as this sounds... I'm now in... Hell?"

"Correct," Karina Reed replied enthusiastically. "Impressive. It usually takes people a lot longer for the realisation to sink in."

The presenter probed further, "Tell me, Corbin... do you remember who killed you?"

After a few moments of hesitation, he simply shook his head. "No. I don't."

"And do you recognise me at all?"

"...No."

"I know I've been off the TV for a while now," Karina teased playfully. "But *that's* just rude."

The audience found this highly amusing, laughing hysterically. They hung on to her every word as she continued, "Not to worry. It'll come to you. Everything should come back to you throughout the evening as we listen to a series of voices. These will be the voices of those who shaped you into the person you are today. Let's kick things off with someone who sounds so ruddy adorable. Do you recognise this cute little voice?"

The speakers crackled before a young boy's voice filled the studio, "I didn't want your money. I wanted your time."

Tears brimmed in Corbin's eyes. "Oliver," he whispered, his voice breaking.

The host's tone was laced with contempt as she remarked, "I'm surprised you recognise your own son's voice, considering the little time you spent with him."

Frantically, Corbin searched through his pockets, a sinking feeling setting in as he realised that something precious was gone. "Where's my wallet?" he exclaimed anxiously. "There's a picture of Oliver in there! I need my wallet."

Karina reassured him, explaining, "Calm down. Whatever you have with you at the time of passing transfers to the afterlife. We've secured your belongings in a locker - including the photo of Oliver."

"Alright," he replied, visibly relieved.

Corbin's memory dragged him back to the day his son was born. The scene unfolded on giant screens for all to witness. In the footage, a nurse, her expression fraught with concern, approached the father. "Mr. Armstrong?" she asked, her tone gentle but heavy with the gravity of her message.

"That's me. How's my wife?"

The nurse paused, her eyes reflecting a deep empathy. "Mr. Armstrong, I have some very troubling news. There were complications from an infection linked to the pregnancy.

Despite all we did, Sarah's condition worsened too quickly to save her. I'm sorry."

People handle grief in many different ways, but few would respond with such cold detachment.

Karina asked her guest, "What did you say to that nurse?"

Corbin avoided the question, yet the screens betrayed him, displaying his reply, "That's certainly inconvenient. Considering the huge amount of money I've paid you people, I expect there'll be some sort of refund?"

The nurse was taken aback by his heartless response.

The audience erupted in boos, and Karina fanned the flames, "That poor boy had no mother, and you could argue that he never had a father either."

Corbin, on the defensive, retorted, "He had the means to get anything he desired. Endless toys. More than most children could even dream of."

"He didn't want or need endless toys. Let's replay the voice clip, shall we?"

Once more, Oliver echoed through the speakers, "I didn't want your money. I wanted your time."

Corbin had never felt so disrespected, and a surge of anger consumed him. As much as he wanted to pounce on Karina and slam her head into the studio floor, he contained the urge, reminded of Bones' imposing presence. Instead, he inhaled deeply, striving for composure. "Look... had I known that Oliver's time on Earth would be so... tragically short, I would have done things differently."

The audience chuckled at the notion, and the host remained sceptical too. "Ten years is hardly brief," she countered. "During that decade, your staff represented you at six Christmas nativity plays, five sports days, and twenty-seven award ceremonies for a myriad of talents that you never helped cultivate."

Karina took a cautious step back, her eyes locked on his as she delivered the blow, "You weren't even by his side when Oliver died."

"I tried to be there," Corbin shot back, his voice a mixture of anger and regret.

Be-Be's eyes gleamed with glee as she watched on from the shadows. The Producer was certain that nearly every tormented soul in Hell would be captivated by this episode, fully aware that as the story unfolded, it would only grow more intense.

The host, demonstrating a touch of empathy, recognised, "Yes, to be fair, you did try your best to make it to the hospital on time, which deserves credit. And if the upcoming guest had helped you, you'd have seen your boy alive."

Right on cue, a male teenager's voice echoed through the studio. "Corbin the Coward... Corbin the Coward," it chanted.

A second memory was presented to the studio on the screens for all to see. This flashback revealed a young, petrified fourteen-year-old Corbin cowering in a classroom corner while Kyle Poe, his equal in age but superior in cruelty, loomed over him. This bully, who just so happened to be the most attractive boy in their year, possessed a towering and formidable presence that surpassed that of anyone else their age.

Today's torment from Kyle was the chant, "Corbin the Coward," which the classroom eagerly joined in with.

The bully, armed with a lit Bunsen burner in one hand and a vial of unknown black liquid in the other, addressed his captive audience, "I'm telling you, this little bitch will do whatever you tell him to do. He doesn't even know if this junk is poison, but Corbin the Coward here will swallow it if you tell him to." His gaze pinned Corbin as he ordered, "Drink it... bitch."

Corbin disregarded the command, instead curling up tighter into himself.

The bully swung the flame menacingly close to Corbin's exposed skin. At each cry of pain from the terrified child, the command was repeated, "Drink it!"

After suffering six searing burns, Corbin yielded. With a trembling hand, he took the vial and drank the black substance while the classroom's chants of "Corbin the Coward," continued.

Kyle laughed, "Who knows, maybe this mysterious liquid will miraculously help you grow a spine."

Back in the present, Karina turned to her eager audience and teased, "Should we invite Kyle Poe to join us on stage?"

A unanimous cry of "Yes!" thundered through the studio.

Kyle entered, now a shadow of his former self; obese, balding, and unkempt. Strangely, he was drenched, with strands of seaweed clinging to him. Every step he took left a muddy, wet footprint in his wake.

As the two men's eyes met, fury ignited, and Bones had to intervene as they lunged at each other with fists flying.

The crowd erupted, their cheers and chants filling the air with a fevered intensity, "Fight! Fight! Fight!"

One of the feral beasts hauled a second chair onto the stage, and Bones, with determined force, pushed both men down into their seats.

Another member of the stage crew gave Kyle a towel to dry himself off. As he patted himself down with it, Karina asked him, "You weren't exactly kind to Corbin in the past, were you?"

Kyle, out of breath, finally managed to let out the words, "I was just trying to toughen him up."

"Bullshit," Corbin cut in sharply.

Karina redirected the focus to the man in the hot seat. "Corbin," she said with piercing intensity. "Can you tell us all why weren't you there when your son needed you the most?"

Corbin, determined not to give in to this grotesque spectacle, remained silent, his mind fighting off the surge of this painful memory. Yet, against his will, the past once again unfolded on the screens for all to see, and the audience watched on, spellbound.

The footage showed the tycoon in the expansive office atop Armstrong Industries. Slumped into his leather chair, the man was drained from consecutive meetings that taxed even his tremendous intellect. Seeking solace, he poured a glass of amber whisky and flicked on the television.

Utilising his company's avant-garde technology, currently under wraps from the public eye, Corbin commanded his remote control, "Play 'Die Hard,' but replace Bruce Willis with Pee-Wee Herman." The screen came alive with this surreal version of the film, Pee-Wee's high-pitched voice delivering the iconic lines, providing the mogul with a bizarre yet amusing spectacle.

In a whimsical mood, Corbin next instructed, "Now put me in place of Pee-Wee," and watched as his likeness appeared onscreen. Content but craving enhancement, he added, "Give me bigger muscles." The screen obliged, and his digital self grew brawnier. "Not bad at all," he mused, a smirk playing on his lips.

But boredom soon struck, and Corbin instead surfed channels, first stumbling upon an advert for a tedious new vacuum cleaner with the voiceover booming, "This thing doesn't just suck up your dust. It plays music. It has a clock on it. It'll hold your water bottle. Heck, it does so much that I wouldn't be surprised if it wrote a script for a hit movie." Corbin's response to this pitch was, "Piss off."

The next channel revealed an interview with Richard Bruce, aka Big Dick. The obese politician smugly explained, "The people of New York City have seen what a positive difference having Big Dick makes. I feel that everyone should benefit from Big Dick, and that's why I might just run for president sometime." A cranky Corbin gave a brief review of this also. "Fuck... right... off!"

On the third and final attempt to find something decent to watch, Karina Reed popped up on the screen. "Now we're talking," he said with the biggest smile on his face. It seemed her guest, Night Protector, was midway through some kind of rant. He was saying sternly, "...whilst you'll happily accept others being tortured and killed in the name of food and sport. You'll happily do this because you've collectively decided that you are the superior species. Well... I've recently decided that I am now the dominant one. I am at the top of the food chain."

It was at this point that Corbin had heard enough. He muted the volume to help keep his focus firmly on the presenter - someone he was, to put it bluntly, obsessed with. Fixated by her beauty, Corbin reached into his desk drawer, retrieving lotion and tissues, his perverted intentions clear. But the scene onscreen took a gruesome turn as Karina's nose collapsed on live television, her agony apparent though muted. "What the actual fuck..." Corbin breathed, aghast.

He was frantically trying to turn up the volume once more for context when his smartphone began to vibrate.

There was an incoming call from his local hospital.

Corbin didn't know this at the time, but he'd missed almost a dozen attempts to be contacted by them that day.

The father was aware that Oliver had been whisked away to a private clinic by his tutor during the morning for what seemed to be a common chest infection, but it was far graver than anyone had anticipated. When Corbin finally answered his phone, the message was clear: if he wanted to be by his son's side whilst the boy was alive, he had to come now.

He sprinted out of that office.

The drawback of running the world's most secure tech company was the layers of security he had to navigate through, each checkpoint a source of frustration, despite his staff just following protocol. In a bid to hasten his exit, he left his phone, watch, and all other electronics at the second of the six checkpoints, praying it would quicken his remaining clearances.

Once free from the building he had personally designed, Corbin jumped into the AI smart car he had also impressively pioneered. He bypassed the safety codes that capped speed limits, pushing the car to its limits in a frantic race against time to see his son.

Whether it was the car's protest against the override or a glitch in its system, the vehicle soon came to an abrupt halt, Corbin's face slamming into the steering wheel, with his nose breaking with the force of the impact. "Fuck," he cursed, as blood began to stream down his face.

He frantically tried to restart the car, but it was futile, and he quickly realised he had no means to call for help having left his belongings at work.

Stepping out of the car, Corbin anxiously waited for the opportunity to wave down a passing vehicle. When this moment finally came, the driver, shockingly, was none other than Kyle - someone he hadn't seen since their school days many years prior.

Kyle stopped and immediately recognised Corbin. He turned to a seductively dressed woman beside him with a smirk and explained, "This is the guy I was just telling you about. I'm driving one of his frickin' cars. Seriously, this brainy freak designed this car." Looking back at Corbin, he enquired, "What's the problem, freak?"

With urgency in his voice, Corbin began, "I've broken down and I need a lift t--"

"Fuck sake," Kyle snapped, cutting him off. "That best not end up happening to my car. I spent a fortune on this thing, as you know full well."

Corbin, growing more desperate, tried to convey the gravity of the situation. "I need a ride to the hosp--"

"Didn't I read somewhere that you're like the sixth wealthiest guy out there?" Kyle interjected, ignoring Corbin's distress.

"The fourth. But please, I need to get to the--"

"Fourth richest man in the world," Kyle scoffed, turning to the woman with a mischievous grin. "Yet here he is, stranded and vulnerable, like the rest of us mere paupers."

He looked Corbin deep in the eyes before concluding, "I'd love to give you a lift to wherever you need to go, but I've already got plans for this beauty to be sucking on my balls in ten minutes from now, and I am not changing those plans for anybody - especially you."

Kyle sped away, revelling in his cruel triumph as he left his victim behind, disappearing into the distance through the rearview mirror.

Nearly fifteen agonising minutes passed before another vehicle finally came into view. Tragically, by the time Corbin reached the hospital, he had missed the chance to see his son alive by mere minutes.

Consumed by sorrow, the father collapsed in tears upon seeing his lifeless child. He was struck by the realisation that he would never witness his son's future and tormented by the awareness that he had rarely been present during his son's past.

For the first time, the studio audience's demeanour softened, and a collective sympathetic "Awwwwwww" filled the room.

Addressing this reaction, Karina interjected, "Perhaps it's best to hear his full story before offering your sympathy." She turned to Corbin and continued, "We will soon delve into your pursuit of revenge against Kyle, but first... let's go to an ad break."

Chapter Two

Billions of irritated viewers grumbled at their screens, frustrated by the interruption and the prospect of enduring a handful of commercials before the story continued.

Among these viewers were two fairly new housemates, Bert, a 12-foot demon, and Arnie, a much shorter human at just five feet three inches tall. The pair often joked about how their names resembled another duo from a popular children's show.

However, these moments of laughter were rare, as Arnie soon discovered that his housemate had a terrifying temper, often leading to violent outbursts.

One of these attacks came as a result of having to sit through the advertisements. The demon began punching at Arnie, who exclaimed, "What the fuck, dude! Seriously, I'm like seven or eight brutal beatings away from reconsidering living with you!"

Taking a deep breath to compose himself, Bert responded sheepishly, "I'm sorry."

The ads kicked off with a depressed, overweight man standing on a set of scales. A voiceover asked the ominous question, "Are you tired of being fat?" The man nodded in agreement as the voice continued, "For just £5.99 per month, we'll send ravenous wild beasts after you. But remember, if they catch you, they will eat you. So, best get running, fatty."

Right on cue, one of these beasts crashed through the window, its appetite for blood evident. The terrified man sprinted for his life as the voiceover concluded, "He'll be shedding calories in no time."

Next up was a movie preview. The opening scene displayed a beautiful young couple sitting across from each other in the dimly lit corner of an ancient tavern, exchanging infatuated looks.

The same voiceover as before declared, "From a director who's still desperately chasing awards, comes yet another Oscar bait, politically-charged period drama."

The young woman's expression was anguished as she confided in her secret lover, "My family will never accept you."

"They have to," he assured her fervently. "Once I tell them how deeply I love you."

"It's not that simple," she sobbed, her eyes brimming with tears. "I come from a long line of duck hunters. And... well... you're... half duck."

Zooming out, the camera revealed the man's upper body to be human, while his lower half was unmistakably duck-like, with his small flippered feet barely clearing the seat.

"I will declare my love for you to your father tonight."

"No," the woman implored. "It's a terrible idea. Especially during duck hunting season."

"But I must."

The scene shifted to the duck-man dashing through a cornfield, dodging bullets from the enraged father.

"Nope," he called out, his comical webbed feet propelling him as swiftly as possible. "He doesn't approve."

The trailer ended with the voiceover promoting the film, "Forbidden Love, coming this August. Just eighty-five dollars to see in cinemas or free on illegal download sites."

Back in the studio, the comedian Cuddles was in his element, heating up the audience with his hellfire humour. "Hey there, sinners and lost souls! How's everyone doing in this eternal barbecue we call home?" His jest was met with cheers and raucous applause.

His routine rolled on, "Since I've been in Hell, I've had my flesh torn apart with hooked chains by some nutter with screws in his face - though try having an actual conversation with the guy and you'll quickly realise a few of those screws are missing. Just about everything here has tried to kill me - tomatoes, dolls, a vagina filled with razor-sharp teeth, a greasy strangler, and even a frickin' telepathic car tyre. I was also recently assaulted by a horny poltergeist as I tried to fall asleep, and when I did finally dose off, I was then tormented by a guy with knives for fingers and a face that made me look like Brad Pitt. Despite all this and more, I'd rather spend an eternity down here in Hell than one weekend back on earth with my mother-in-law."

The audience erupted into fits of laughter, the punchline hitting its mark perfectly.

Cuddles reached for a bottle of water by his feet and took a leisurely, large sip, relishing that sweet sound of admiration.

Meanwhile, offstage in the darkness, Be-Be was quietly conversing with Karina Reed. "Everything okay?" she asked, her face etched with worry.

"I think so," came the host's reply.

"You sure? If this interview is too close to home, I can find someone to continue the show, or I could step in t--"

"No," Karina cut in firmly. "I need to be the one who's staring him down once he realises that he's the reason I'm dead."

"Alright. If you're certain."

"I am," she affirmed before making her way back to the stage.

Be-Be was about to return to her own position when her eyes caught a shadowy figure lurking just a few metres away.

Whoever it was, slowly began to walk towards her. "This area is off-limits to the public," Be-Be announced.

The figure remained silent as it continued its slow, deliberate approach.

"You shouldn't be here. Do I need to call security?"

Yet again, there was no reply.

The glare of the studio's lights eventually illuminated the figure before Be-Be. It turned out to be the old woman who had earlier cast a piercing gaze in her direction during the show. Summoning her exceptional mind-control skills, Be-Be attempted to compel the intruder, "Go back to your seat."

"I shall do no such thing," the woman replied firmly.

For more than three decades, Be-Be's mind-bending abilities had never met resistance, but this woman stood unaffected, impervious to her mental command.

Confronted with what seemed like a whole new type of enigma, Be-Be was at a loss. She prided herself on reading people - knowing their essence from the slightest gesture or shift in posture. Yet now, mere steps away, Be-Be could not discern a single thing. With a mix of fatigue and trepidation, she posed the question, "Who are you?" her voice laden with a hesitation that betrayed her usual confidence, uncertain if she was prepared for the actual truth.

"For now, all you need to know is that I'm your superior," came the cryptic reply.

"I answer to no one," Be-Be retorted firmly.

"Everyone answers to someone. And as your superior, I wanted to personally express my gratitude for your time and efforts as the ruler of Hell. However, your services are no longer required. We have a replacement prepared to assume the role."

"Who?" Be-Be demanded.

"Not *who*. *What*."

Chapter Three

Camp Diamond Water was a place steeped in legend. Countless stories were told regarding the massacre that took place there almost a decade prior. Rumours and conspiracies became more absurd when, despite its dark history, the camp reopened to the public, only to then witness a new wave of inexplicable killings. According to police reports, the second tragedy was seemingly unrelated to the first. So... was it the work of a copycat killer, or could something more sinister, like demonic possession, be at play? These were just two of the many popular theories circulating.

A few years back, the campsite had been declared legally off-limits to visitors. Despite this, rebellious youths, such as Baz Poe, his girlfriend Lexy, and lifelong friend Mark, would often disregard the rules and venture into the forbidden grounds.

During one of their visits, the crackle of the fire, alongside the gentle lapping of the lake's water against the shore, created a haunting symphony beneath a blanket of stars. Illuminated by the amber glow of the flames and the luminous moon, these three teens huddled close, revelling in the thrill of being somewhere with such a dark history.

Beside them was their worn-out tent that the group consistently promised to replace after every rainy camping trip, which invariably left them drenched. Despite their pledges, they never took action and so here it was yet again.

In a moment spurred by the solitude enveloping them, Baz posed a thought-provoking question, "Imagine being the last human on this planet. What would you do?"

Mark quipped, "No people means no pussy, so I'd have to end it all. What's the point in carrying on if you aren't getting any pussy?"

With a mischievous grin, Lexy playfully retorted, "Well you've lasted this long without it."

Her boyfriend couldn't help but burst into laughter, while Mark offered a strained smile, his pride stung.

After a brief reflection, Lexy unveiled her apocalyptic bucket list, "I'd be first in line at every rollercoaster in every theme park."

Mark couldn't resist the opportunity for his own witty comeback, "And who exactly would be operating those rides for you, Einstein?"

"Fair point," she laughed, but Lexy's joyful expression quickly morphed into one of sheer alarm.

This sudden shift caught her boyfriend off guard, prompting him to ask, "Everything okay?"

Struck mute by her fright, she could only gesture frantically towards the lake's opposite bank.

Their eyes widened in shared terror at the sight of a shadowy figure brandishing a sizable knife. Baz, attempting to diffuse the tension, assured, "Don't worry, it'll be some kid fucking with us. I've heard they do it a lot here. I prepared for it."

With a dash to their tent, he emerged brandishing an even larger blade, and bellowed across the water, "You call that a knife? This is a knife!"

Mark joked, "Take it easy, Crocodile Dundee."

The stranger across the lake, unfazed, began a slow and deliberate trek around its edge, heading straight for the group.

Lexy's anxiety skyrocketed, "He's coming right for us."

"Let him," Mark stated, feigning bravado, though his voice betrayed him with a hint of genuine concern. "Three against one. He wouldn't stand a chance."

As the ominous figure drew closer still, Baz projected a threatening warning across the distance, "Take one more step and you'll regret it. I'll stab ya!"

In defiance of the warning, the figure continued to draw nearer until his face was aglow with the fire's light, revealing a young boy.

It was almost comical how frail and harmless he appeared. With a slender build, tousled blonde hair, and large, innocent blue eyes, he wouldn't have looked out of place being cast as Oliver Twist.

Mark let out a breath of relief. "You were right," he said. "It's just some little kid."

Baz abandoned his facade of composure, unable to mask his fear any longer. "He may be a kid, but that doesn't make the knife he's holding any less deadly."

The trio began to retreat, with the boyfriend brandishing his own blade in a menacing stance, not giving up hope on being able to scare off the stranger.

Lexy broke down into hysterical sobs. "You said it would be someone playing a prank on us."

"I thought it was," Baz panicked. "But clearly not. This psycho clearly intends to harm us."

Shifting his focus to the boy, he bellowed, "And we'll defend ourselves if we have to! I will fucking stab you!"

However, like the first warning, this one failed to deter the boy. On the contrary, with a chilling thirst for violence in his eyes, he pointed his knife forward and advanced toward the teens at a far greater speed, screaming like the deranged individual he was.

Lexi and Mark fled as fast as their legs could carry them, with the girlfriend pleading to her partner, "Kill him!"

Adrenaline coursed through Baz as he made the split-second decision to comply. Matching the assailant's fervour, he advanced toward him. Both were driven by a desire for retribution, but it was the boyfriend who delivered the fatal blow, plunging his blade directly into the assailant's chest.

The young boy locked eyes with Baz with an expression of utter despair across his face. His once innocent blue eyes soon turned red with blood. With his last breath, he murmured, "It was a joke," before falling to the ground.

Lexi and Mark witnessed the entire scene, halting their flight and instead gazing at the fallen boy, stunned.

"What have you done?" Lexi asked, her voice tinged with panic.

"I did exactly what you fucking told me to do," Baz snapped back.

The trio encircled the boy, their regret palpable. Mark struggled to contain his emotions and asked, "What do we do now?"

The one responsible for this terrible deed, fighting back his tears, ordered, "We dispose of the body and we never mention this again."

Still overcome with panic, Lexi sobbed, "My mother will see right through me. She knew something was wrong after I stole a packet of crisps at the self-service checkout. I think she'd know something was fucking wrong if I were to dispose of a child's body."

Without hesitation, Baz retorted, "Then I'll have to kill you too."

A heavy silence fell.

The girlfriend couldn't bring herself to fight or even flee. She was paralyzed by terror.

After a short while, her boyfriend unexpectedly burst into laughter, causing a great deal of confusion.

"What's happening right now?" Lexi managed to utter amidst her sobs.

To everyone's shock, the supposedly dead child began to laugh also.

This only intensified the bewildering atmosphere.

"It's a *joke*," Baz revealed, still chuckling as the young boy stood up.

"A joke?" Mark responded sceptically whilst hyperventilating. "That makes zero fucking sense. There's a knife stuck in his fucking chest."

"He's *fine*," Baz assured.

Still utterly baffled, though slightly relieved, Lexi asked her boyfriend, "So... who the fuck is he?"

"Not *who* the fuck. *What* the fuck."

Chapter Four

Kyle went on to recount the unexpected visit his father had received just days earlier. It was Corbin, one of the wealthiest men in the world whom his father had bullied throughout their childhood, standing just a few feet away. But why?

Imagine Kyle's astonishment when he saw that standing beside Corbin was Oliver, the very boy who was now at Camp Diamond Water with the teens.

Kyle was dumbfounded. He had heard rumours of the boy's passing, so how he was standing there at that moment was utterly perplexing.

Breaking the silence, Corbin asked, "Do you know what happened on the day I last saw you? The day you drove away from me."

"I do," came the hesitant reply. "I heard you talk about it on the tele."

"Well... having known what happened to me that day, I wasn't sure if you wanted to apologise to me. Very few have my number, so I thought perhaps you had difficulty reaching me."

"I have nothing to apologise for," Kyle said curtly. "I'm not a mind reader. How was I supposed to know that you were trying to get to the hospital?"

"True," Corbin sighed, disappointed by the response.

At that moment, Kyle was unaware that his lack of remorse had just determined his fate.

The billionaire continued, "I wanted to show you that there were no hard feelings by giving you a gift."

"I'm hoping that gift is your latest car model, to make up for that older piece of shit model I'm stuck with?"

"Not quite," Corbin chuckled. "I'm giving you this. His name is Oliver and if you'd like him... he's yours."

With that, the young boy stepped forward and with a smile, said, "It's lovely to meet you."

Kyle looked puzzled. "You're giving me some random boy that not only looks like your dead son but shares the same name? Like... what... did you search for a kid that looks like yours and buy him?"

"No. I created him. I built him. Believe it or not, he's not human. He's so much better than that. He's a free babysitter, a cleaner, driver, hairdresser, chef, dentist, doctor, and more. Heck, it does so much that I wouldn't be surprised if it wrote a script for a hit movie. This artificial genius will make your life so much easier, you'll soon wonder how you ever managed without him. I envision a future where every single household will have one of these, and I want you to have the first."

"He's... a robot?"

"It's more technical than that, but essentially, yes."

Kyle curiously poked the boy on his cheek to see if he could feel the metal - which he could. "And will these things all look like your dead son?"

"No. I was going through a bit of a crisis when I designed this particular one. But I'm over that now and ready to move on."

Hesitantly, Kyle confirmed, "Okay, I guess I'll take it."

The boy looked up towards his new owner with a smile and said, "Hello, my new father."

"*Nope*," Kyle snapped. "That's too weird!"

Corbin reassured, "Tell him that it's weird. Let him know what you'd rather be called, and he'll call you it."

"Okay," came the hesitant response. "So... does this thing come with instructions?"

"No, it's all setup. Just talk to it, and it will talk back."

The sceptical man was unsure as to whether this monstrosity was for him, but ultimately accepted the gift - figuring he could always sell it on to someone else if things didn't work out. "Thanks... I *guess*?"

"Enjoy," Corbin concluded before making his way back to his vehicle.

As promised, Oliver was more than willing to perform a variety of tasks. The boy cooked, cleaned, walked the dog, built a guest house - after personally obtaining the legal permission to do so - and even sensitively presented his owner with a cancer diagnosis, which, following a hospital appointment with x-rays, turned out to be accurate.

Things took a strange turn when Kyle was having an intimate encounter with a neighbour. Midway through, he emerged from beneath the sheets and was startled to see Oliver standing there holding a plate with two bacon sandwiches.

Kyle's lover was also taken aback. "Who the fuck is *this*?" she exclaimed, catching her breath.

"I'll explain later," he replied.

With a creepy smile, the boy said, "I thought you might want some sandwiches after you're done."

"Well... that's fucking strange," Kyle told him. "You need to leave this room *now*."

As Oliver complied, the man quickly added, "But leave the sandwiches."

The situation took an even weirder turn when the couple were saying their goodbyes at the front door. The woman told Kyle, "That was amazing. I've never orgasmed so hard."

Suddenly, Oliver emerged from the next room and announced, "Her body language and tone indicate that she's not being truthful."

Embarrassed, the neighbour asked, "Seriously, *who* is this kid?" She turned to her lover and insisted, "I swear, you made me cum like three times."

"She didn't," Oliver stated confidently. "Perhaps I can give you the top ten tips on how to pleasure a woman according to an article in the latest Heels and Hilarity magazine?"

"No," Kyle snapped, mortified.

The woman awkwardly said, "I'm going to go now. I'll text you later," and hastily made her escape.

At that moment, Baz Poe came rushing down the stairs with a large rucksack. "Alright, I'm off to the campsite," he announced.

The father had a sudden idea. "Why don't you take Oliver with you?"

"The *robot*?" the son replied, taken aback. "Why?"

"There's apparently nothing he can't do. He could put up your tent, handle your fishing, build a raft - or even build a bloomin' three-story hut if you wanted him to."

In reality, the man was actually hoping to have more sex that night and didn't want to be embarrassed by the machine yet again.

After a few moments of hesitation, the boy shrugged, "Sure," and it was during their journey to Camp Diamond Water that Baz came up with the plan to prank his mate and girlfriend.

As always, "Oliver was more than happy to comply."

After being fully briefed on the events that led to this moment, Lexi and Mark gazed at the young boy in amazement.

Mark asked, "How have you never mentioned before that you own a frickin' robot?"

"I don't know. It's kind of cool, I *guess*. But it's not like the latest PlayStation or anything like that."

Lexi added, "What is wrong with you? This is *way* cooler than any gaming console. The possibilities of what we could do with this thing are endless."

"Like what?" her boyfriend asked.

Mark giggled before saying, "I have an idea."

He proceeded to whisper into Oliver's ear before leaning back to enjoy the show. A few seconds passed before the robot emitted what sounded like a comically loud and prolonged fart.

Naturally, the trio found this hilarious, and even Oliver laughed along with them.

As the chuckles subsided, Baz said, "You know, this thing identified cancer in my Dad."

"That's amazing," Lexi responded with enthusiasm, then paused, realising her insensitive choice of words. "I mean, it's amazing that it's so smart - not the cancer part."

Her boyfriend mused, "You think it could figure out a cure for cancer if we asked it to?"

"Probably," Mark chimed in. "But first... maybe we can make it fart some more?"

"*Absolutely*," Baz and Lexi replied in unison.

Throughout the remainder of the night and into the early hours of the morning, the teenagers continued in this immature manner until they eventually began drifting off to sleep inside their tent.

Baz, the last to succumb to slumber, noticed that the tears in the tent were larger than he had remembered.

He whispered, "Oliver."

From outside, the boy whispered back, "*Yes*?"

"Is it going to rain tonight?"

"There's a 65% chance of rain in approximately two hours from now."

"Any chance you can do something to keep the rain from pouring into our tent?"

"Sure. I've got this."

Oliver sat outside, his eyes fixed on the horizon, a mischievous grin spreading across his face. He had just the plan.

When Baz woke again four hours later, the rain was indeed pelting down. True to his word, Oliver had kept the interior dry.

A sigh of relief escaped Baz as he settled back down, only to freeze as he realized Lexi and Mark were no longer beside him.

It seemed strange that both of them would leave the tent simultaneously at such an early hour, especially under a downpour.

Calling out, he asked, "Oliver?"

The response came, "*Yes?*"

"Are Lexi and Mark out there with you?"

"They *are*, yes."

Confused by this unexpected turn of events, Baz asked, "What are they up to?"

"Just... hanging out."

Something didn't feel right. Going against his gut instinct, the boy zipped open the tent to investigate further.

Amidst the familiar scents of the lake and damp grass, a more unsettling metallic odour, that of blood, mingled in the air.

Baz's apprehension deepened at this unexpected smell. "So... where are they?" he asked apprehensively.

Still sat, relaxing away, Oliver simply pointed towards the top of the tent.

The weary teen examined some kind of fabric that his new toy had used to shield them from the rain as requested.

It resembled leather at first glance.

Upon further inspection, Baz's heart lurched in his chest. It was unmistakably the skin of Lexi and Mark, stretched out and repurposed. The face of his girlfriend was staring right at him, frozen in an expression of unimaginable terror.

Panic seized the teen as he vomited beside the murderer, who seemed unfazed by the chaos, still calmly gazing towards the lake as if the night remained serene.

In a blind rage, Baz grabbed his blade and lunged at Oliver, whose reactions were chillingly precise. In a flash, the blade was in Oliver's grasp, and he secured Baz's arm in a vice-like grip, the sound of a cracking bone slicing through the air.

Baz's screams tore through the night. He desperately pleaded, "Please! Stop!"

"I will," Oliver murmured with a sinister calmness to his voice. "Soon enough, anyway."

The artificially intelligent psychopath drove the knife's edge perilously close to, but deliberately missing Baz's heart, instilling a raw terror in the victim's eyes.

Oliver instructed, "I've steered clear of your vital blood vessels. Press hard on the wound, and perhaps you'll linger long enough for your father to witness your last breath."

Two hours slipped by before Kyle's phone shattered the silence of the early morning.

"Who the *fuck* is calling at this time?" he roared.

His initial fury at the intrusion was swiftly replaced by dread as the voice on the line urgently summoned him to the hospital due to his son's dire emergency.

Never before had the man left the house with such speed.

Behind the wheel, Kyle pressed the accelerator to its limit, cursing the vehicle's inability to defy the laws of speed.

Each ticking second felt like an eternity as he willed the car to go faster.

"*Come on!*" he pleaded.

Many thoughts raced through the father's mind. Why was his son rushed to the hospital when Oliver was capable of handling anything they could and more? And why hadn't this robotic freak contacted him personally to explain the situation? Things just weren't adding up.

Suspicions of foul play intensified as the vehicle itself suddenly took full control, swerving to the side of the road before the engine sputtered to a halt.

"*No!*" he yelled, frantically attempting to restart the car, but to no avail.

A glimmer of hope appeared as headlights approached in the distance. In a race against time, Kyle tugged on the door handle, intending to seek the driver's help, but the door remained stubbornly shut. The father's heart sank as the car cruised by with Corbin behind the wheel, sporting the biggest, most smug grin imaginable.

The realisation hit him like a ton of bricks.

This *whole* ordeal was an act of revenge.

Years of enduring bullying had come full circle, and now he found himself on the receiving end. Corbin had found a way of inflicting extreme pain, without even lifting a finger.

Kyle frantically retrieved his smartphone from his pocket, hoping to call a friend for assistance, but each button pressed yielded no response.

In a fit of rage, Kyle punched the steering wheel repeatedly with all his strength, and with one of those blows, the engine roared back to life.

The man, somewhat sceptical, pressed his foot on the pedal, not truly believing the car would start moving. He assumed this was all part of the twisted mind games.

However, it surged forward. He was back in control.

To his surprise, Kyle even made it to the hospital.

The father parked mere inches away from the entrance doors, narrowly avoiding crashing straight through the glass. The desperation to be by his son's side couldn't have been more evident.

He tugged at the door handle with urgent force, but, once again, it stubbornly remained shut.

"Son of a *bitch*," Kyle screamed.

He desperately tried the other doors, and with each failed attempt to get out, the more hopeless he felt. But the distraught man knew that he couldn't just give up.

In a last-ditch effort, he slammed his entire body against the windscreen glass, before kicking away at it with all his might.

Again, this was to no avail - with not even one single crack emerging.

The car's engine suddenly sprang to life by its own accord, jolting Kyle into an upright position.

"Thank god," he whispered with a hopefulness that was to be short-lived.

He frantically tested the doors and even with the vehicle running, they remained sealed shut.

It was at this moment that any little hope Kyle had was extinguished.

The vehicle began to inch itself forward and veered away from the hospital where the son lay helpless. Kyle, now a truly broken man, could do nothing but watch on as the building shrank into the distance.

The car's movements were deliberate, navigating with unsettling purpose. Its integrated voice system cut through the silence, "Now playing your new playlist... songs to die to." The opening bass line of 'Another One Bites the Dust' by Queen filled the vehicle - an ironically cruel jab at Kyle's situation.

The second track was 'The End' by The Doors, twisting the knife in his torment. It was during this song that the headlights revealed Corbin and Oliver standing ahead by a vast lake, their grins wide and chilling in the gloom.

By this point, Kyle wasn't at all surprised to see them. He had expected it.

The car rolled to a smooth halt beside them, the window lowering just enough for a sinister exchange.

"Oliver's projections were spot on, as usual," Corbin said calmly. "Your son's fight ended just a few seconds ago."

"You're a sick *fuck*!" Kyle screamed, his voice raw with fury.

Corbin's laugh was cold and dismissive. "A simple apology might have spared you and your son's life."

"All this because I didn't fucking *apologise*?" Kyle's voice cracked, tears streaming down his face. "I swear, I will fucking *kill you*! You and your... *toy*!"

As the car began a slow descent backwards into the lake, Kyle's fate was sealed. "Wait! I'm *sorry*!" he pleaded, panic lacing his voice.

But Corbin remained silent, sharing a look of triumph with Oliver as the car sank deeper into the murky depths.

"I'm *sorry*!" came one final desperate plea.

Water seeped through the window's narrow opening just as 'Highway to Hell' by AC/DC erupted from the speakers. Moments later, the song and Kyle's cries were muffled by the engulfing lake.

Once the car had fully disappeared, Corbin turned to Oliver with a nonchalance that belied the atrocity they had just committed. "There's something we need to discuss," he said, his voice still eerily calm.

"What would that be?" Oliver responded.

"You would have turned thirty today," Corbin mused. "I think it's time we gave you a new look and a few upgrades. How does that sound?"

"Sure thing, Father. I'll do whatever you say."

Chapter Five

Be-Be threw her all into trying to crack the mystery of exactly who the stranger was that stood before her. Despite her best efforts though, she hit a brick wall.

The usual master manipulator heaved a defeated sigh. "We should chat after the show."

"*Now* will be just fine," the self-proclaimed top dog shot back.

Confident enough that Karina Reed had the show under control, Be-Be suggested, "How about we grab a drink in the Green Room?"

"Lead the way."

As they navigated the labyrinthine backstage, Be-Be couldn't help but pry. "You could at least throw me a bone and tell me your name. I'd quite like to know who exactly is firing me."

"Fine. Funnily enough... I too am called BB."

"*Really?*"

"Yes. It's short for 'Bad Bitch'. It's what they started calling me as I climbed the corporate ladder, throwing down any dead wood on my way up. I hated the name at first, but it grew on me."

"So... Bad Bitch, what did I do wrong? If you tell me, maybe I can switch things up a bit."

The elderly woman let out a laugh. "Doubtful," she said. "Even if you met me halfway, you'd still fall short of the ruler my team and I have in mind for Hell. It was bad enough when Satan felt the need to get creative and started tailoring punishments to each individual sinner, but whatever - they were being punished nonetheless. But *you*! *Your* methods feel like more of a treat. Trips to the circus. Television entertainment. It's all flamboyant nonsense, and it stops *today*."

"I don't quite see it that way," Be-Be said carefully, trying not to upset the woman too much. "It's kind of like a rehabilitation process, where we reward good behaviour."

"*No!*" Bad Bitch roared. "It's kind of like one big party that everyone seems to be invited to."

"Again, that's not how I see it," Be-Be countered, her voice steady yet remaining cautious.

If only she knew what awaited them in the Green Room, Be-Be might not have been so sure of herself. As she pushed the door open, her jaw hit the floor. The room was a circus of drunken buffoonery.

Feral beasts were throwing down in a wild poker game, tossing around human limbs instead of chips.

"Limbo!" bellowed Napoleon, the diminutive French leader, with the intention of using his short height to his advantage in the game. Be-Be and Bad Bitch watched on as demons bent and twisted in grotesque ways, ducking under a limbo stick made from a live snake, to the cheers of a rowdy crowd.

In the far corner, a brawl erupted between Saddam Hussein and Joseph Stalin: both notorious for their ruthless reigns. Their ego-fuelled debates often turned physical.

Bad Bitch arched an eyebrow and said in a condescending tone, "Not a party, huh?"

"*Enough*! Everybody *out*!" Be-Be yelled, her tone leaving little room for argument. She might play around, but crossing her was a bad idea - a fact that almost entirely cleared the room out within seconds.

However, one defiant figure remained where he was, undeterred by the order.

Raising his head defiantly, Napoleon addressed the women with unwavering confidence. "I'm staying right *here*," he declared. "And there's *nothing* you can do to make me leave."

Before Be-Be could respond, Bad Bitch took the lead. With a chilling smile, she shattered a beer bottle with a swift motion. She used the jagged edge to deliver a fatal blow to the former French leader's throat.

As Napoleon's eyes widened in shock and he gasped for breath, the man fell lifeless to the ground.

Bad Bitch's actions did not end there. With mysterious power, she placed her hand on his neck, miraculously healing his wound and bringing the man back to life. But before he could comprehend what had happened, she swiftly used the broken bottle to pierce his heart, extinguishing his life once more.

The woman, with a chilling demeanour, was toying with her prey. She used her miraculous skills to next mend Napoleon's wounded heart, bringing him back from the dead yet again.

"I could keep this game going *all night*," she taunted. "Or... you can piss off."

Overwhelmed with fear and confusion, he nodded vigorously before hastily fleeing the scene.

Choosing not to visibly acknowledge Bad Bitch's extreme behaviour, Be-Be simply nonchalantly enquired, "Can I offer you some refreshments?"

"No, thank you," came the reply.

"Are you sure? Maybe just a glass of water?" Be-Be persisted.

Bad Bitch's expression suddenly turned to one of alarm. "You have water here?" she asked, her voice strangely tinged with fear.

Perplexed by this reaction to such a common question, Be-Be responded tentatively, "*Yes*? Is that a problem?"

"Perhaps not if you were the ruler of Heaven," Bad Bitch replied fiercely. "But this is *Hell*. We embrace *fire*, not *water*. Get rid of it. All of it!"

Be-Be nodded slowly, taken aback by the intensity of the demand. "Sure."

Back at the main stage, Karina had almost concluded her segment with Kyle. She turned to him and asked, "Before we let you go, any chance you'd like to offer Corbin just one sincere apology?"

The man responded with a defiant "*No*."

Karina smirked in response, "As expected," drawing a round of chuckles from the audience. "Well then, it's back to the lake for you."

Right on cue, the stage floor suddenly split, revealing a pit from which murky waters erupted. Kyle uttered a desperate "*Wait*," but was swiftly submerged along with his chair into the aquatic abyss below.

Subsequently, Bones brought forward two additional chairs onto the stage as the crack sealed itself back up just as miraculously.

Karina, moving the show forward, asked, "Corbin, do you recognise this next voice?"

A disgruntled male retorted, "You *lied*! You need to come clean to my family!"

Shaking her head playfully, Karina teased, "He sounds angry. Making friends doesn't seem to be your forte, does it?"

"He was a *very* good friend... *before* his betrayal," Corbin retorted coldly.

"Oh, so you know who it is then? Let's welcome to the stage... Duncan Perry."

The studio lights flickered and the audience cheered as a tall, nerdy-looking man with a wiry frame and thick-framed glasses stormed onto the set. His eyes blazed with fury, and his usually mild-mannered facial expression was twisted into a scowl of utter disdain.

He strode purposefully as his steps echoed across the polished floor. When just a few feet away from Corbin, Bones stepped in to keep them apart, firmly instructing, "Take a seat. *Now*!"

Duncan complied without challenging the imposing figure before him, but he struggled to get comfortable on the chair. He was strangely unable to lean back and couldn't figure out why. As he stretched his arms out behind him, the man was alarmed to discover that a sharp steak knife had been stabbed into his back at some point. Despite his best efforts, he couldn't quite reach far enough to grab it.

"Allow me," Bones said as pulled the weapon out.

"Thank you," Duncan replied before turning his attention back to Corbin. "How could you? You've ruined my name!"

"How could you betray me?" Corbin, always the victim, shot back.

Holding her hand up, Karina interjected, "Let's put a pin in that for now. Sharp-eyed viewers might've noticed an empty chair. Surely we're not spoiling you with two guests at once?"

Facing the camera with a playful smirk, she teased, "Whose seat could this be?"

Taking that seat herself, Karina revealed with a dramatic flair, "It's *mine*, you mother fucker."

Gasps came from the crowd as the host continued, "You still don't seem to remember me, but you *will*. And you'll give me answers. Unless you want to find out how Bones got his nickname, you'll give both Duncan and me answers... right after the commercial break."

Chapter Six

The abrupt pause in the drama left viewers even more on the edge of their seats than before, their frustration clear.

Once again, Bert, the 12-foot demon who was watching from home, struggled to control his aggression. With razor-sharp claws, he viciously attacked his housemate, Arnie, causing fresh wounds and leaving him heavily bleeding. Arnie, in serious pain, sighed, "Come on, man. Seriously? I swear, I'm like six or seven brutal beatings away from reconsidering living with you."

Realising he'd gone too far, the embarrassed demon responded, "I apologise."

They awkwardly watched on as the first advertisement began. It revealed a woman reclining in a bathtub filled with blood-red ice. A voiceover cut through the unsettling imagery, asking, "Tired of men pursuing you for just one thing... your kidneys for the black market?"

The woman exaggeratedly nodded in response.

The voice continued, "Then it's time for you to try the brand new online dating app, 'Our Soul Dating.' We put our soul into ensuring that not all our members are complete psychopaths. With nearly 60% of our subscribers surviving their dates, it's no wonder that 'Our Soul Dating' is the number one choice for so many."

Following the ad, a film teaser rolled out, featuring a sour-faced elderly woman glaring out of her kitchen window.

The same voiceover as before boomed, "Meet Coral Bleek - a bitter old woman who takes great pleasure in tormenting the residents of Werrington Village."

The camera shifted to her intense gaze upon an eight-year-old girl being questioned by police at her lemonade stand. As that stand is forcibly closed down, Coral cackled, "Consider this a lesson for illicit trading on my territory."

Another snippet showed the insufferable woman interrogating her village's Facebook group, seeking out the identity of whoever allowed their dog to defecate on her street - receiving no response. After conducting an all-night stakeout, she nabbed the guilty party. Soon after, the dog owners' shock was palpable when they later received a mysterious parcel containing the "returned goods."

We next see a young couple, Aiden and Donna, who are sharing a kiss. Trouble loomed as the voiceover revealed, "Tragically, this poor girl is Coral's daughter."

The image shifted to Coral's harsh ultimatum to the boy, "End the relationship now. You'll never be worthy of my girl."

The final clip depicted a visibly distraught Aiden confiding in his friend, Jane. "I can't believe she would end the relationship just because her mother told her to do so."

As 'A Christmas Carol' played softly in the background, inspiration struck, "What if we staged our own Christmas Carol scenario?" he continued. "I think we could do it. It wouldn't just be about getting Donna back. We would be avenging the entire village for the misery her mother has caused."

Donna, intrigued, declared, "That's the most ludicrous idea I've ever heard. So, naturally, I'm in."

The trailer concluded with the voiceover summing up, "A Christmas Coral is coming straight to televisions this December... since let's be real, nobody's going to spend money to watch this shit."

Whilst the remaining commercials played, Cuddles engaged with the studio audience in his usual manner. "I do miss a couple of things from my time on Earth," he reflected. "Like being able to order a steak without the only choices being overcooked or charred beyond recognition."

The audience let out amused laughter before he went on, "Just the other day, I told a doctor that I felt burnt out, and he replied, 'Of course you are. You're in Hell. That's the ambience here!'"

Reaching the end of his set, the comedian announced, "The rest of our show promises to be a wild ride, and it'll start again real soon. Enjoy!"

Amid the crowd's applause, Cuddles approached Bones and asked about Be-Be's whereabouts.

"Beats me. I've been wondering the same thing," Bones replied with a shrug.

"I'll go look for her," Cuddles volunteered. "And if I'm not back before the next ad break, you can entertain the crowd."

Bones chuckled in disbelief, "Very funny. Could you imagine?"

After a few moments of awkward silence, he prodded further, "You're joking, *right*?"

"There will be a bloodbath if this audience isn't constantly entertained."

With that, the comedian picked up his bottled water and began to walk away.

"Wait, you're not serious," Bones called out, his voice tinged with panic. "Cuddles! You're joking, *right*? I don't do jokes!"

Chapter Seven

Years had slipped by since Corbin had ended Kyle's life in that lake. The image of his foe's body submerged in the water used to cross his mind daily. Over time, it became a less frequent memory. Months had passed without giving him a single thought... until today.

Seated in his office, Corbin proudly gazed at an article on his laptop declaring him the wealthiest man in the world. He wished dearly that his former adversary could have been alive to witness this monumental moment. Nonetheless, he took pleasure in knowing that this story would still likely have reached anyone else who had tormented him during his school years. After all, the headline was practically everywhere.

Corbin scrolled through the comments section beneath the story. The narcissistic part of him anticipated an outpouring of support and admiration. However, to his genuine surprise, the majority of messages were filled with hatred towards him.

Amidst the negativity, one comment in particular caught his eye. A user named 'YoMomma69' had this to say: "I witnessed this coward in a club, instructing his security to physically slap about anyone attempting to engage with him -

except for the attractive women, of course. Such a tough prick when hiding behind real men, built like brick shithouses."

Two aspects of this comment hit a nerve with Corbin. Firstly, he loathed being labelled a coward. It ignited a fire within him and triggered memories of being taunted with that same word during his experiences with being bullied. The second point of contention was the identity of the commenter. YoMomma69 had surfaced multiple times over the years. He was, in modern terms, what youngsters would refer to as a "hater."

Corbin reached out to a newspaper featuring the same headline, an image of his face occupying half the front page. He showed it to Oliver, now embodied as a handsome, well-groomed thirty-year-old man, who stood motionless in the corner of the room. "It's funny," the recently minted trillionaire remarked to his creation. "My life revolves around technology, yet there's something special about the tactile experience of holding paper in your hands."

After a brief pause, Corbin enquired, "Are you proud of me?"

Oliver sprang to life. "Of course," he affirmed.

"In that case, say it," Corbin requested.

"I'm proud of you, Father."

"Thank you."

The man retrieved a wallet from his pocket and carefully unfolded it to look at his photograph of the real Oliver. Having his flesh and blood by his side on this adventure would have been incredibly meaningful to him, but it remained a dream unfulfilled.

Swiftly concealing the picture once more, Corbin suppressed his emotions. He didn't want to become too overwhelmed with feelings, especially when he was just minutes away from meeting his celebrity crush.

Yes, Karina Reed had finally agreed to interview the trillionaire after numerous rejections over the years. Surprisingly, it wasn't his status as the 'richest man in the world' that had influenced her decision. The television personality was eager to interview the mastermind behind the world's first artificial intelligent entity in the running for president.

Initially perceived as a ludicrous concept by just about everyone, Oliver's charisma and ability to say the right things to the right people quickly won over the public.

He became a beloved figure, but could people truly accept him as their leader? The answer to this question would unfold in the upcoming evening's lively televised debate, where he and his opposing candidate would face off.

Corbin's dear friend and employee, Duncan Perry, burst into the office with a grin, "I knew you'd be holding that newspaper."

Corbin shot back with a smile, "Just until I find a frame for it."

The atmosphere shifted as Duncan got down to business, "I know you've got your big interview soon, but I wanted to catch you before tonight's debate, so now's probably my only chance. I made something for you. I officially completed it last night."

He placed a trigger device featuring a yellow button on Corbin's desk. Initially, it had a red button, but research indicated that people were always inclined to press a red button whenever they saw one. This creation was also equipped with a cover to prevent accidental activation of the trigger.

Corbin's mood turned. "This best not be what I think it is," he grumbled.

Duncan quickly explained, "I thought it'd be better to have it and not need it than need it and not have it."

Corbin's anger rose. "I told you to drop this project. This is *not* what I pay you to do?"

"I did this in my own time at home, with my own money."

With a stern look, Corbin ordered, "Oliver... destroy it!"

The robotic entity looked puzzled. "Destroy the device or destroy the human?" came the reply, causing understandable unease for Duncan.

"What the fuck?" he said fearfully.

Corbin chuckled, "He's *joking*." In truth though, he was uncertain whether it was actually in jest, and therefore confirmed, "Destroy the *device*."

Duncan rushed to defend his work. "Hold on! Millions will be watching tonight. Oliver's never had a glitch or gone rogue, but it's surely just a matter of time till he does. And what if that moment just so happens to be this evening, with all those *millions* of eyes on him? Pressing this button won't kill him; it'll merely shut him down temporarily."

The appeal fell on deaf ears as Oliver seized and effortlessly squashed the device, reducing it to scrap.

Duncan couldn't be certain, but he thought he detected a faint scowl cross Oliver's features whilst this had happened.

Corbin's voice cut through, sharp and cold, "You've been watching too many Terminator movies. My faith in Oliver surpasses any human I've met in my lifetime. Your gadget is an insult to me, my enterprise, and to Oliver himself."

Duncan exhaled a weary breath, "My intentions weren't to offend." He paused, then, "Look... there's something else I need to give you."

"*What?*"

From his pocket, Duncan produced an envelope, which Corbin inspected with swift scrutiny, only to cast it aside seconds later.

"You claim to not want to offend," Corbin seethed, "and then present me with *this*?"

"I assumed you'd be happy for me. I'll be running an entire company. It's a *huge* opportunity for me."

"Well, *I assumed* you'd be happy with a paycheck that dwarfs 99% of all other workers on this planet. I thought you'd be happy with unlimited leave. I thought you'd be happy with the luxury sports car I gifted you just a few days ago as a thank you for your hard work."

"I was - no, I *am* happy with all those things. I truly appreciate all that you've done for me. This is just something I feel I need to do. As my friend, I hoped you'd understand and support me."

The silence spoke volumes. With a heavy heart, Duncan concluded, "My last week happens to be at the same time as our employee retreat. Hopefully, you'll still allow me to attend. It could be a nice way for me to say goodbye to people."

"I'm sorry but the retreat is exclusively for th--"

Their exchange was cut short by a knock at the door.

"What is it?" Corbin called out with a furious tone.

A young female television producer timidly opened the door and explained, "Mr Armstrong, we've almost finished setting up the studio next door and Miss Reed has just arrived."

"I'll be there in just a moment," Corbin responded before diverting his attention back to Duncan. "Get out of my sight."

The trillionaire was confident that his spirits would lift upon sharing a space with Karina Reed. His fascination with her had spanned years, during which time he had devoted endless hours to studying video clips and gazing at her images in magazines.

In anticipation of their meeting, Corbin had wondered if Karina would be charmed to discover that he had engineered an artificial likeness of her to keep him company at home and even help him settle in for the night. He often considered himself a visionary, foreseeing a future where such practices would be commonplace. Still, he recognised that she might not currently share his enthusiasm for the concept - especially as Karina's demeanour in person seemed unexpectedly cold.

Facing away from her guest, she shouted into her phone, "That lying bastard promised he would accept the new offer."

Throughout several minutes of her call, she failed to so much as glance at Corbin, much to his frustration.

When the conversation finally came to an end, she seemed to continue to deliberately avoid looking at him. "A power play?" he pondered. "Playing hard to get?"

As the production team adjusted the lighting, Corbin took the initiative to break the ice. With a hint of arrogance, he posed, "This must be quite an intimidating moment for you?"

Her gaze reluctantly met his as she retorted, "And what makes you say that?"

"Well," he said with a conceited grin, "You're about to interview the richest man on the planet."

"I think I'll manage," Karina chuckled. "I've interviewed just about everyone during my career. Lil Problemz, Miss Judy Lawrence, and let's not forget those exclusive interviews with the world's first Superhero - or supervillain, depending on your perception of him. So, yeah, I think I'll be okay."

"Ah, yes," the trillionaire responded awkwardly. "I saw what Night Protector did to that face of yours. That whole ordeal must have been terrifying."

"Yes. It was."

"Well, I'm glad the surgery I funded was so successful."

Karina looked taken aback. "Wait," she said wearily. "*You* were my mystery donor?"

"Yep. I was outraged that someone could wreck such a pretty face."

"Um, *thanks*?" she replied, not quite sure what to make of this revelation.

A crew member announced, "Cameras are rolling, and we're ready whenever you are, Miss Reed."

The presenter gathered herself and asked the guest, "Good to go?"

"Let's do this."

Despite Karina's lingering discomfort over the revolution of this stranger's generous payout, she masked her unease with practised poise. Facing the camera with a sudden sunny disposition, she announced, "Today, I have the honour of sitting with the mastermind behind Oliver Armstrong. It's delightful to have you here."

"The pleasure is entirely mine," he replied with a smile.

"First off, I'm curious about the seriousness of your proposition to have artificial intelligence govern our fine nation, and if you ever anticipated getting this far in the presidential race?"

Corbin leaned in slightly, the corners of his mouth hinting at a smirk. "I approach all my endeavours with gravity," he said. "Although I must confess, I never expected the public to warm to Oliver quite so quickly."

Karina's gaze sharpened, hanging on every word as Corbin elaborated, "Perhaps I shouldn't have been surprised though. Initially, my team saw Oliver as just a thing - nothing more than a machine. Then, a poignant shift occurred when a grieving employee sought solace in Oliver after her father had died, feeling a deeper spiritual connection with him over everyone else within the organisation. Now, Oliver is not just a fixture in the office; he's a cherished friend, attending socials, and milestones, and he even stood as the Best Man at a senior manager's wedding. For the few sceptics left who are still unsure of Oliver, I invite you to watch tonight's debate with an open mind. If his words don't sway you, I'll eat my hat."

Karina replied with a playful jab, "You're certainly in a position to buy another hat."

A chuckle escaped Corbin as Karina pressed on, "Some argue that this presidential race is nothing but a publicity stunt and one that's played a part in your ascent as the world's wealthiest individual. What's your response to these people?"

Corbin's demeanour softened into a mischievous grin as he retorted, "I'd tell them to go eat a bag of dicks."

Karina's piercing disapproval was evident, accompanied by an acidic tone as she continued, "Your ethics are frequently scrutinised. Many would contend that you are not a particularly pleasant individual - and that's putting it nicely. Given that Oliver was created by you, it's likely that he also shares your questionable ethics, is it not?"

Corbin appeared surprised. "I was under the impression that this would be a puff piece," he remarked.

"Let's all take a comfort break," Karina frustratingly called out to her team.

"A bag of dicks?" she sneered once the cameras were off. "Very classy, Mr Armstrong!"

"I panicked," he explained. "I wasn't prepared for these kind of questions. Throw me them again and I'll give you better answers."

Karina simply sighed, diverting her attention away from him, and instead towards a small compact mirror.

As the host perfected her hair, Corbin tentatively offered, "If I behave myself for the rest of the interview, perhaps I can be rewarded by having you join me for lunch afterwards, at this amazing and insanely expensive restaurant I know?"

Karina's response was swift, "I'll pass."

His reaction was one of bruised pride. "If it's a matter of money," he grumbled, "I can cover it."

Karina's reflection in the mirror vanished as she faced the man with contempt. "Do you think that I need your money? You don't think that I make enough on my own?"

"I was merely offering reassurance," Corbin replied, flustered.

"Well I'm reassuring you, my finances are more than adequate."

She couldn't leave it at that. "In fact," she said sternly. "I'm currently in the process of trying to buy the biggest apartment in my block for *three times* the amount it's worth - simply because I *can*."

Her voice softened as she concluded, "Though it now seems I may have to wait for the old stubborn current owner to die before that happens."

"Fingers crossed the bastard has a heart attack real soon," Corbin joked.

The presenter showed no response to the attempt at humour. With renewed determination, she directed her crew, saying, "Let's get this show on the road, people! Maybe the coward can start answering some difficult questions."

As the crew hastened their preparations in the background, Corbin silently reminded himself, "I'm *not* a coward."

The word lingered in his thoughts for the rest of the interview, leading to brief responses just to expedite the process.

When it did finally conclude, Karina hurriedly left the set without so much as a "Thank you for your time" or "Goodbye," leaving the trillionaire even more embarrassed and infuriated.

"Bitch," he muttered.

It wasn't long after this departure that the celebrity found herself browsing some shop aisles for her evening dinner, primarily selecting bottles of red wine.

Accustomed to the spotlight, Karina always basked in the glances and whispers of recognition from passersby. It irked her then when a young female cashier didn't give that classic double-take. This absence of familiar attention only compounded the embarrassment when the cashier, with a hint of impatience in her voice, declared, "Your credit card has been declined."

"*Excuse me*?" Karina's voice wavered with disbelief. "That can't be right. Run it again, please."

With an audible sigh and an exaggerated eye roll, the cashier swiped the card once more, only to be met with the same rejection.

A flush of anxiety rose in Karina's cheeks as she scanned the store, praying the moment had gone unnoticed by onlookers. Taking another card from her purse, she requested in a mortified tone, "Try this one."

Despite being an entirely different card linked to an entirely different bank account, it was once again declined.

Humiliated, she pleaded to the shop worker, "This has to be an issue with your card machine. I have plenty of money. I'm pretty famous."

"Okay," the cashier grumbled, uninterested.

Karina grabbed one of her bottles of wine. "See," she insisted, her voice tinged with desperation. "My face is literally right here on the label."

"That's *great*," the response came sarcastically. "But what I need is the face of Andrew Jackson... on a twenty dollar bill."

"*Yes*," Karina snapped. "I got the reference."

Suddenly, a new card was extended from behind her. Karina spun around to find Corbin standing there, his grin easy and calm as he told the cashier, "I'll cover this."

The employee's demeanour transformed instantly, her voice infused with enthusiasm, "Absolutely, Corbin Armstrong!" She was practically trembling as she took the card from his hand.

Karina stood mute, overtaken not by awe - she had made her lack of adoration abundantly clear during their previous encounter - but by the sinking realisation that this was likely no random encounter. Corbin had surely tracked her down, and what's more, she was convinced he had orchestrated her current predicament. This notion solidified when the cashier returned the card to Corbin with a self-satisfied air, stating, "That went through just fine. I guess our card machine isn't the problem after all."

"You're welcome, Miss Reed," the trillionaire said smugly. "Oh, and I've also made arrangements to get you into your new apartment real soon - a little thank you for seeing me today."

With that, he exited the store with a playful skip in his step.

Karina was unsure about the true meaning behind his cryptic words. He had previously covered her medical expenses, but could he have also purchased a home for her? She prayed for that not to be the case. She wanted no gift from that man.

As the celebrity was being driven back home, the feeling of unease intensified with every turn of the wheels.

When the driver eventually drew close to the luxurious tower block where she lived, the disturbing sight of an ambulance parked ominously at the entrance sent her heart into her throat. "What have you done?" she whispered, a shadow of dread passing over her.

She hurried to the doorman, her voice urgent, "What's happened?"

His face was etched with sorrow as he replied, "It's Mr Deagon. He's had a heart attack."

"Is he going to be okay?"

"It doesn't look promising."

As if on cue, paramedics emerged, wheeling a stretcher that bore the unmistakable shape of a human form shrouded in a sheet.

The doorman lowered his head in a silent tribute, while Karina succumbed to the emotions. "Oh, God, no," she cried.

Tears streamed down her face as a troubling thought lingered in her mind. Could this be what Corbin had hinted at in the store? Despite his unsettling ways, he couldn't be responsible for someone's death, could he? Karina dreaded the possibility that she had undermined a psychopath's sense of control, leading him to display, in a chilling manner, the extremes he was prepared to go to establish his dominance and exhibit his power.

And if that were indeed the case, it deeply concerned Karina that this deranged individual could potentially be the mastermind pulling the strings behind the nation's next leader.

Chapter Eight

More than one hundred million viewers were glued to their screens for the spectacle of the century - a presidential debate with a twist. The nation was abuzz with a question that felt more at home in a sci-fi thriller than the political arena: Could a being of silicon and circuitry legitimately replace the flesh-and-blood commander-in-chief?

In an arena that was a dazzling array of lights and anticipation, the live audience was a sea of eager faces, rippling with excitement.

Into this electric atmosphere bounced a young and attractive female host.

She pirouetted onto the stage, her high heels clicking a rhythm of confidence as she positioned herself between two starkly empty podiums. These were the soon-to-be battlegrounds for the candidates, who would vigorously pitch their future visions in a bid to win the hearts and votes of the American people.

Flashing a camera-ready smile, she chirped, "Good evening... I'm Karina Reeve."

It wasn't just her name that bore a striking resemblance to the other television icon - Karina Reed. From her voluptuous curves to the fiery cascade of red hair that bounced in a hypnotic dance with every step, she was uncannily similar. Yet, Reeve revelled in the one distinction that set them apart - youth. She continued to purr into the camera, her voice a melody of mischief. "Please don't go confusing me with Karina Reed."

A ripple of laughter surged from the crowd, and she rode that wave with gleeful ease. "That happens to me all the time," she smirked. "So, let me explain how you can tell us apart. You can find pictures of Reed online without her makeup, and it's like her face and body have thrown a wrinkle party that everyone is invited to - they're everywhere, like the notorious spaghetti junction in China. As for me," she paused, a twinkle of scandal in her eyes, "The only lines I've had on my body was when a world-famous footballer snorted cocaine off my bare ass."

The audience roared with laughter, the sound booming like thunder, much like in Hell, where Reed's own audience was tuned in through the studio's monitors. Their giggles however were promptly extinguished as the offended host bellowed, "It's *not* funny!"

Corbin's memory reclaimed the narrative, with Reeve returning to the script. "Well, aren't we a lively bunch tonight?" she beamed, her voice a symphony of warmth. "But let's focus, people. I'm about to introduce to the stage your potential future leaders. One of these individuals will shape our great nation during the next few years and beyond. But before we let them battle it out, let's take a peek at their promotional videos, shall we?" With a flourish, she gestured to the screens, and the audience leaned in with anticipation.

As the lights dimmed, the monitors came to life with footage of Oliver Armstrong, his silhouette advancing in a deliberate, cinematic pace towards the camera. A voice, both soothing and assertive, resounded from the speakers, "To the great people of America, you have embraced our nation's progress, already accelerated by the innovations of Armstrong Industries."

The video presented a series of uplifting moments. It opened with a surgeon, once left without work following a severe industrial incident that cost him an arm. Fast forward, and there he stood anew, his bionic arm operating with astonishing speed and precision. Next came footage of the U.S. military, now outflanking all rivals, empowered by robotic limbs that enabled them to leap over daunting barriers and perform feats of superheroic scale; their enhanced capabilities a testament to their newly augmented might. Athletes, too, were breaking records with extraordinary finesse and velocity, ushering in an unprecedented age of human achievement.

The narration pressed on, "But this is just the beginning for this great country. Oliver Armstrong pledges to elevate our nation, empowering every American to achieve feats once thought impossible."

With that, the shadowy figure in the video finally revealed itself as Oliver, donning a t-shirt with the words 'Making great even greater.'

The crowd rose, delivering a thunderous ovation as the real Oliver briskly made his way to the stage, assuming his place at the podium. Despite the logical assumption that this artificial entity could not truly experience human sentiment,

Oliver seemed to be genuinely moved by the continued adoration he received, going as far as wiping a genuine tear.

Then the focus shifted to his rival. The video showed Richard Bruce, aka Big Dick, majestically sitting upon a horse, clutching an assault rifle in one hand and a beer in the other, dressed in a suit made entirely of American flags. The voiceover boldly proclaimed, "America, unparalleled yet unfulfilled... until now. Once you have Big Dick, you'll never want to go back."

With that brazen claim, he swaggered to his podium amidst a surge of applause, the flag-themed suit his armour.

Reeve cut straight to the chase, "Big Dick, what's your six-month plan for America?"

He grinned, "Simple. More guns, less immigration. More meat, less salad."

His answers were met with cheers, and he pressed on, "More horses, less pathetic tiny dogs that look like rats."

He seized the mic from its stand, his speech gaining momentum. "Who loves warm apple pie, like the kind momma used to make?"

A resounding "Me!" echoed back.

"Big Dick means smaller prices for warm apple pies like momma used to make," he declared, cocky as the crowd ate up every syllable. He turned to Oliver, taunting, "What's up?" and theatrically dropped the mic.

Oliver retorted with a smirk, "What's up? Well, not your penis."

The audience and his rival both froze at the jarring jest.

Oliver elaborated, "Isn't it ironic that somebody that calls themself 'Big Dick' struggles to rise to the occasion?"

On cue, the screens flashed with an image of Viagra pills labelled to 'Richard Bruce.'

The embarrassed candidate scrambled to recover, "There's thousands of Richard Bruces out there. Could be any one of them."

But the monitors zoomed out, revealing the infamous American flag suit beside the pills, as laughter cascaded through the audience.

Big Dick's face flushed red as Oliver pressed on, "Limp Dick here is all bark, with no bite. He may seduce you with sweet nothings written by his expensive PR team, but I've seen his true colours. And it's time you did, too."

Suddenly, a new clip began to play, showing Big Dick in a candid moment. During his promotional tour, he looked out to a crowd of adoring fans and snarled, "Look at all these morons. I swear, sometimes I'm ashamed to be called an American. It's too bad Night Protector didn't wipe us all out before he disappeared."

A frantic producer buzzed into Reeve's earpiece, "Where's this footage coming from? It's not our end."

Reeve, puzzled, whispered back, "I have no idea."

"We can't stop it!"

On-screen, Big Dick's contempt continued, "They'll swallow any drivel I spout. I bet I could win their votes with just the promise of a free hot dog – which hopefully they'd choke on."

Boos erupted from the crowd as Big Dick protested, "I didn't say half of that!" His defence went unheard as someone, or something had muted his microphone.

Surprisingly, these pleas were the truth.

The footage was a masterful AI fabrication, indistinguishable from reality even by the sharpest experts.

Oliver concluded his onslaught, "America deserves a leader of integrity, not one peddling falsehoods. I may be unconventional, but perhaps it's time for a different kind of president. Someone who's not in it for self-interest. Someone who won't deceive you. Someone who'll fulfil their promises. And I promise that voting for me means voting for every American. No more crumbling family businesses, no more hunger, no more homelessness. I can foresee our nation's path with either of us as president - one future is grim, where only a few prosper at everyone's expense. The other is a certainty; a future where our great America will be even greater. That future can be ours - if I have your vote."

The audience's applause thundered once more, leaving Big Dick a diminished figure, his usual swagger washed away by the tides of scandal.

Karina Reed and Duncan Perry were tuned into the live debate from their respective homes, gripped by a palpable sense of impending doom. Meanwhile, their future selves in the depths of hell were rewatching the reconstruction on the studio monitors, their hearts burdened by even greater sorrow as they knew too well of the extreme pain and suffering that was to follow.

Chapter Nine

There are specific occasions when it is deemed socially acceptable to consume alcohol in the early hours of the morning. These instances include being at the airport before embarking on a holiday, as well as during Christmas and birthdays. You might also argue that being an employee at the world's most successful company, led by the world's most richest man, who was instrumental in creating the world's first artificial president certainly warranted celebration, even at such an early hour.

As part of the Armstrong Industries annual employee retreat, a magnificent ballroom was a spectacle of luxury, hosting nearly 300 enthusiastic and highly intoxicated guests.

To celebrate the imminent arrival of the president himself, numerous American flags adorned the walls.

Below them, a brass band filled the room with infectious rhythms, and the space was electrified by the performances of daring acrobats and professional dancers.

Due to the predominantly male makeup of the company, a substantial number of flirtatious women were paid to attend the party and mix with the men.

Waitstaff moved through the crowd with trays offering complimentary a-class drugs, which the guests eagerly indulged in, despite most of them having never taken anything stronger than paracetamol before this moment.

Additional secluded areas were also available, including a room dedicated to numerous hot tubs, where the understanding was that whatever occurred within them would remain confidential.

Another room could only be described as a sex dungeon. It contained an assortment of S&M paraphernalia, such as whips, chains, and leather restraints, which were scattered around and hung from hooks on the walls. Many attendees, completely unfamiliar with this environment, would stumble in and initially giggle to themselves like naughty schoolchildren. They would cautiously examine the equipment like cavemen discovering fire. Some picked up the whips with a mix of fascination and confusion, while others curiously attempted to fasten the leather restraints around their wrists in a puzzled manner.

This type of extreme social gathering was entirely new to almost every single attendee at the retreat, including Corbin himself, who had chosen to organise things this way under the mistaken belief that this was simply how all the filthy rich partied. It would be fair to say that his repeated viewings of The Wolf of Wall Street had also sparked some inspiration. Nonetheless, attendees were lapping it all up.

One of the very few sober members of the team, Joshua, was taken aback by the increasingly wild scenes unfolding before him. He approached a colleague who appeared equally shocked and remarked, "Shit's got a little bit crazy."

"It has," came the reply. "I'd usually be eating cornflakes and reading the paper at this time.

"Same. By the way, I'm Joshua."

"Chris," the man said as they shook hands.

Out of nowhere, another male colleague beside them suddenly pulled both his trousers and underwear down, revealing a nipple tassel on each of his testicles. Whilst witnessing this drunk man comedically spinning them around, Chris commented in a disgusted tone, "I'd rather be at home eating the cornflakes."

"Yup," Joshua replied. "That's terrible behaviour from the head of Human Resources."

With a sigh, he continued, "This is a lot more extreme compared to last year's retreat."

"I wasn't with the company last year. What did you all get up to?"

"We had a pretty epic Dungeons and Dragons tournament," Joshua recalled. "Oh, and some karaoke."

"Just a tad different then," Chris laughed.

"Yup. I can see why all phones and devices were taken from us. Imagine if footage of this got out. The media would have a field day. Especially as the President is supposedly joining us at some point."

This grand ballroom stood at the centre of Ivy Village, a self-sufficient miniature town reserved exclusively for Armstrong Industries staff, situated miles away from civilisation. It provided ample housing for all employees for their company retreats. The village also offered water sports at its artificial beach, a well-stocked store, shooting range, spa, fancy Michelin-starred restaurants, and a casual greasy spoon diner for those with less expensive tastes. Not that anyone ever had to put their hands in their pockets, as everything within Ivy Village was complimentary.

Seated in the diner, far enough from the chaos taking place within the ballroom, was Corbin. Most of the patrons around him appeared to be in good spirits, engaging in lively conversations and singing along to the songs playing from the jukebox. Amidst the clatter of dishes, laughter also resonated from the kitchen. The only person who didn't appear to be having a good time was the trillionaire himself. He was too preoccupied to even acknowledge the waitress as she set his steak and eggs on the table, along with a large, gleaming steak knife.

Corbin's distraction originated from a few factors. Firstly, he had come across a comment on his phone that had infuriated him. Whilst reading an article announcing Oliver as the new president of the United States, his infamous hater, 'YoMomma69', had left a comment that read, "That awkward moment when our country is being led by a freak of nature designed by an unhinged twat. What could go wrong."

"Ugh, fuck off," Corbin muttered quietly as he closed his phone screen.

Another reason for his agitation stemmed from the impending need to make a decision that had been weighing on his mind for weeks. There was something he felt compelled to do for the sake of his business, yet he was uncertain as to whether he could go through with it.

The jingle of bells signalled the arrival of an awkward-looking Duncan Perry as he entered through the door. He hesitantly took a seat at Corbin's table and tried to lighten the mood with a joke, "Steak for breakfast? You've changed."

"I could say the same for you," Corbin retorted. "Friends don't stab each other in the back."

"I'm sorry you still feel that way."

Corbin took a moment to collect himself before adopting a more sombre tone. With a look of regret on his face, he earnestly stated, "I'm sorry. I'm just being selfish. Of course, I support you."

Surprised by the sudden change of tone, Duncan replied, "Okay... *thank you*."

"That being said--"

"Here we go," Duncan frustratingly interjected.

"No, no... please, indulge me with just one attempt to convince you to stay."

"Alright. Go for it."

"Well... I have no illusions that Armstrong Industries owes much of its success to you. Since the day we met, I've envied your abilities. The more skilled you became, the harder I worked to keep up. You inspired my drive, which ultimately led to me becoming the richest person in the world, and I believe that you deserve to be the second richest."

Sliding a cheque across the table, he concluded, "This is my offer. This is what I'm willing to pay to persuade you to stay."

Duncan was taken aback by the number of zeroes written on it. He took a moment to gather his thoughts before responding, "That's very generous but--"

"*Generous*?" Corbin laughed. "It's *mental*. I'll probably need to pass some kind of sanity test just to get this approved. I wouldn't be surprised if there's a police investigation to ensure that this decision isn't against my will because nobody in their right mind would give away this much money - but I'm willing to do just that to get you to stay."

"Here's the thing," Duncan said awkwardly. "I don't like things being handed to me on a platter."

"I didn't hear you complaining about that sports car."

"I'm not complaining about anything. I'm just trying to explain that I value hard work. *Earning* decent pay gives me a sense of pride and purpose. What I need is a new challenge... not free money."

With that, Duncan slid the cheque back.

An uncomfortable silence filled the air before Corbin reluctantly admitted, "Here's the thing... I can't let you go."

"Sorry, *what*?" Duncan replied, clearly taken aback by the sheer audacity and sense of entitlement. "That's not your decision to make."

"No, it is," the boss stated with a sinister undertone. "You know too much. You've been a big part of this company since day one. That's a lot of years and a lot of secrets that I wouldn't want to get out. So... sorry... but, no, I can't let you go."

Duncan looked at his former friend in utter disbelief. "You really have changed," he said. "Who the *fuck* do you think you are?"

The soon-to-be ex-employee rose to leave, and Corbin furiously bellowed, "Sit the fuck *down*!"

Embarrassed by the scene unfolding, Duncan scanned his surroundings. He found it strange that not a single person in the diner had reacted to this sudden outburst. He concluded that nobody wanted to upset their boss by staring, but it was still unsettling to see not one natural reaction.

Struggling against his usual gentle nature, Duncan sternly told his boss, "I'm leaving. Right now. And there's *nothing* you can do about it."

"I could kill you," came the louder response, which yet again, not one single person reacted to.

Shaken, Duncan tried to conceal his fear and retorted, "You're going to *threaten* me? In front of all these *witnesses*?"

Corbin locked eyes with him and sneered, "Witnesses? What witnesses?"

As though responding to some invisible signal, each patron became unnervingly still, then in a chillingly synchronised manner, they turned their heads away from the men.

Fear gripped Duncan, mixed with sheer confusion. This collective behaviour was far from ordinary, even among the most dedicated of workers.

The grim truth washed over him.

With a heavy heart, Duncan posed a question, though the answer already weighed on his mind. "They're all... like Oliver, aren't they?"

A silent nod was Corbin's only reply.

Desperation took hold, and Duncan bolted toward the exit, only to find his path obstructed by the synthetic beings. He zigzagged between the tables, desperate to escape, but it was futile. They not only thwarted his every attempt but also converged upon him, herding him into a corner.

A flicker of hope sparked within the man. He had come prepared with something he never truly believed he'd need to use. It was pure chance.

From his pocket, he withdrew another trigger device, crafted hastily after the first was destroyed by Oliver months prior. Should it work as intended, a single press would short-circuit every android within a mile radius.

With a deep breath, he pressed the button.

But there was no miraculous shutdown, no saving grace.

A dreadful realisation struck him. He had neglected to insert the batteries. "*Fuck*!"

The synthetic predators lunged.

Duncan fought with all his strength, but it was no match for their overpowering force. They pinned him down, his chest slammed against the surface of Corbin's table.

The trillionaire picked up his steak knife and uttered, "You should have accepted my offer."

Duncan wriggled desperately but couldn't budge. With tears flowing down his cheeks, his sobs turned into screams of agony as the knife plunged into his back.

Turning to the waitress, Corbin casually requested, "Could you be a dear and fetch me another knife for my breakfast?"

"Of course," she replied before heading into the kitchen.

As his old friend bled to death, Corbin addressed his remaining creations. "I literally can't trust anyone," he told them. "If my best friend was willing to leave me, what's to stop these other assholes from doing the same? And don't get me wrong, I don't need them. Just one of you gets more work done than a thousand of them. But they know too much - and fuck knows what they'd end up disclosing to my competition."

He took a moment to consider his options before issuing a chilling command, "Kill them. Kill them all."

Chapter Ten

Thirty of Corbin's creations were parading around Ivy Village in human form.

Although one might assume that the tech genius had constructed all of them himself, that was not the case. He had only personally built Oliver, who, in turn, could create others at a much faster rate. These subsequent creations were capable of producing even more, leading to a rapid increase in numbers.

It was clear that these creations surpassed any human with whatever task was presented to them. If they were to be ordered to build their own army - make no mistake that this could be accomplished within a single day.

The order for these machines was a simple one: exterminate every human, other than Corbin, within Ivy Village. Some selected firearms, hefting assault rifles with mechanical precision, while others opted for sharp knives from the numerous eateries. A select few relied solely on their formidable physical prowess. Systematically, they advanced towards the ballroom.

Inside, the music throbbed through the room, its pulsing beat matching the frenzied heartbeats of the partygoers. Joshua and Chris were still deep in conversation, their camaraderie rooted in a mutual appreciation for Japanese culture.

Joshua raised his voice over the music. "Seriously," he shouted. "Any place that celebrates Christmas with KFC is top tier in my book."

"I know, right," Chris concurred, his smile matching Joshua's enthusiasm.

"And my girlfriend's dying to visit the rabbit island there - she adores them."

"Yup. That's on my list too. So, what does your girlfriend do for a living?"

"She's in construction."

"That sounds tough, probably quite a challenging atmosphere for a woman, I'd imagine?"

"It used to be, yeah. It's changed a lot though. There are still some dinosaurs with old-fashioned ideas but--"

Abruptly, Chris's words halted, and he froze, leaving Joshua perplexed but too courteous to press, attributing the pause to a possible medical issue or nervous habit.

When the silence stretched too thin, Joshua attempted to steer the conversation forward. "And what about y--". His words were cut short as Chris's hands wrapped around his neck in a swift, violent embrace.

Panic flared in Joshua's eyes as he frantically scanned the room for help, only to realise the commotion of inebriated partygoers and the sensory overload of the festivities concealed Chris's lethal intentions.

Joshua struggled in vain against the steel-like grip of his assailant, his punches ineffective against the unyielding form.

Chris was eerily expressionless as he delivered his chilling apology, "Sorry. Orders from above," before the final, gruesome sound of a neck snapping echoed above the surrounding commotion.

As Joshua's lifeless body slumped to the ground, Chris released his hold and emotionlessly sought out his next target.

In the side room filled with the luxurious hot tubs, the atmosphere was already stiflingly hot - more so when the maximum temperature limit was overridden. It quickly spiked to an unbearable level. The heat became suffocating, causing the partygoers to gasp for air, their skin turning red as they desperately fled from the scalding water, only to find themselves facing a new horror.

Every one of the synthetic entities, sleek and deadly, had now infiltrated the party.

One such machine, devoid of emotion, rhythmically discharged an assault rifle into the crowd, syncing its gunfire with the beat of the music. It did so with a twisted playfulness, as though mocking the gravity of the carnage it wrought. Each burst of gunfire saw more partygoers collapse to the ground.

It wasn't long before the musicians halted, stunned into silence as the staff realised the grave danger they were in. The once vibrant music gave way to the sound of sheer panic.

Chris stood guard by the exit, grabbing panicked victims as they tried to flee. He used his inhuman speed and strength to swiftly break their necks with chilling efficiency. The sickening crack of bone echoed through the room as bodies fell lifelessly to the floor one after another, their screams abruptly silenced.

In the dungeon-themed room, a different synthetic predator attempted to whip a captive to death, but the tool failed to inflict harm due to its gentle material. Frustrated by its ineffectiveness, the machine, in a fit of rage, jammed the whip's handle down the victim's throat instead.

Not even the musical instruments were spared from becoming implements of slaughter. A brass cylinder was hurled with lethal precision, decapitating a guest, while another's skull was brutally caved in by being forced into a trombone.

The air was thick with the scent of fear and blood, and the glittering lights now illuminated a scene of horror beyond imagination. The killers, devoid of mercy or remorse, continued their relentless onslaught, turning the party of the century into a blood-soaked nightmare until all were lifeless.

Corbin was acutely aware that when the news of this killing spree was to emerge publicly, managing a believable false narrative would be a complex task. Nevertheless, he had a general sense of how things should play out. With his deep understanding of technology and human behaviour, he often laughed at the gullibility of the masses online - how millions would uncritically accept information being presented to them, errors and all, from dubious sources without the slightest effort to verify the facts. Now, consider how many more people would believe fake news if the online content or televised reports appeared genuinely authentic.

Corbin's technological prowess gave him an edge. He knew that one day there would be a future where seeing and hearing could no longer be equated with believing, especially online and on television - even amongst the most gullible. He foresaw a world where video and audio could be so masterfully altered that the truth could only be verified through direct, in-person experience. How was he so sure of this dire future? He was to be the architect of it. He had already developed the means to create such convincing fabrications - even using it publicly once already during the presidential debate. It was this very innovation that he intended to use in an attempt to get away with his heinous crimes.

To initiate the process, Corbin called Oliver. Upon receiving a response, he declared, "We're moving forward with the plan. Find me some scapegoats."

After concluding the conversation, the trillionaire let out a tense sigh. "Could this work?" he pondered.

As part of his plan, Corbin had to create the impression that he too was a victim of the brutal attack. Merely being injured wouldn't suffice when everyone else had been so savagely murdered. He figured that he had to be seen by people barely alive.

Still seated in the diner, the man beckoned the waitress and said, "I'm sorry to sound like a broken record, but I'm going to need another knife."

She brought one over, and Corbin continued, "I'm also going to need you to stab me, multiple times - six or seven. But I must stress, do *not* kill me. Avoid all major arteries."

"You got it, boss," came the reply. "Should I also box up the rest of your steak for you?"

"No, thank you. Just the stabbing."

As the waitress was about to plunge the knife into his flesh, he quickly panicked, "Wait! Wait! Wait! Make it three or four times."

"You got it, boss."

She went to stab him for a second time, and just like before, he freaked out at the last second. "*Wait*!" he shouted. "Just once will be fine."

The subsequent phase of the operation hinged on Oliver and his exceptional ability to persuade.

Concealed within a secure chamber, the president sat across from five Nigerian men, having just explained their potential roles in Corbin's scheme, promising them substantial rewards for their cooperation.

One of the men asserted, "But we are not terrorists. I wouldn't even swat a fly."

"It doesn't matter whether you are terrorists or not," Oliver countered. "Your looks fit the profile, and in the eyes of this narrow-minded society, that's sufficient enough for our plan."

A second Nigerian, gripped by anxiety, voiced his concern, "If we agree to this, our children will think we're monsters."

"Your children will be set for life - which is surely more important? Imagine a life for them beyond their wildest dreams: clean water to drink, safety from violence, and the freedom to live anywhere and pursue anything. This is the future you'll be providing for them if you simply consent."

After a hushed conference between them, one of the men meekly conveyed their reluctant agreement, "Alright. We'll do it."

Oliver's lips curled into a satisfied smirk as he warned, "*Great*. But don't forget, should you retract your commitment or stray from the agreed path in any way, not only will your families not receive a single penny from us... but we will kill them."

Chapter Eleven

In Hell, Karina Reed and Duncan glared at Corbin in disdain having just seen the footage from the Ivy Village massacre. He sat there with his head bowed, resembling a misbehaved schoolboy. "I have a theory," the host declared. "I believe that the association of conspiracy theories with eccentric individuals in tin foil hats is not a mere coincidence. It's a deliberate strategy orchestrated by influential and corrupt figures like you to discourage ordinary people from questioning the status quo. You want them to be too fearful of being labelled as crazy for merely expressing doubts. I am certain that when your story came to light, not everyone believed it, but many chose to remain silent for fear of being dismissed as "conspiracy nuts"."

The studio monitors next displayed a news report featuring Reed's professional rival, Karina Reeve. Once again, she was taunting, "No, I'm not Reed - although I understand the confusion. Here's how you can differentiate between us." Pointing to herself, she remarked, "One of us is a natural redhead." Then, pointing away, she added, "And the other dyes her hair. Now... speaking of dying, news has just emerged of a terrorist attack that took place in Ivy Village, where Armstrong Industries company retreat was being held. Nearly three hundred employees sadly lost their lives. To their friends and family, I'd like to sincerely say... sos."

The news channel aired what appeared to be genuine footage of terrified victims hiding and tearfully saying their goodbyes to their loved ones as the five Nigerian men carried out their brutal attack. The storyline presented consistent footage from various angles, but not a single clip was authentic.

Taking the narrative towards the fantastical, another piece of "recovered footage" showed a terrorist filming himself as he stabbed Corbin, then addressing the camera with a chilling message, "We've just wounded this man. However, we will not hesitate to kill him like the others unless we receive one hundred million US dollars. Without the payment, this will only be the start. More Americans will die and we wi--."

Oliver's dramatic arrival culminated in the swift termination of the terrorist, mid-sentence, as he hurled the band's brass cylinder directly into the villain's chest, the American flag visible in its gleaming reflection. This iconic moment, often dubbed as 'the money shot', left a lasting impression on all who witnessed it.

The president navigated the ensuing chaos with a blend of cinematic heroism and precision, taking down the attackers through a series of stylish confrontations - engaging in hand-to-hand combat, using shards of glass from the scene as weapons, and even turning one of the terrorists' guns against them. After dispatching these killers, Oliver reached Corbin, tending to his wound with one hand while grabbing the terrorist's camera with the other, issuing his own bold warning, "If anyone watching this wants to go after the great American people... keep in mind, you'll have to go through me first."

The presentation of the footage was so convincingly realistic that almost every viewer was completely absorbed by the fabricated story. Indeed, given the authenticity with which it was presented, it's understandable why many would accept it as truth.

As a result of this deception, Corbin, the true psychopath behind so much death, was now depicted as a victim. Meanwhile, Oliver became an acclaimed hero. His impassioned warning, captured on camera for millions to see, had ignited a sense of patriotism in many who had previously been sceptical of him. He now had the entire country eating out of the palm of his hand.

In Hell, the studio audience and those watching the show from their homes were in shock that Corbin was able to effortlessly get away with such a heinous act.

The presenter asked the twisted man, "Why did you choose a different narrative for Duncan?"

Corbin nonchalantly shrugged as he gazed at his enraged ex-friend, who wanted to do him harm. However, Duncan restrained himself, mindful of Bones' watchful eye.

Viewers were shown footage of what appeared to be Duncan recording himself on his smartphone, whilst driving his sports car well beyond the speed limit. To make matters worse, he was being kissed and caressed by a woman who was not his wife. Initially laughing and cheering, his demeanour quickly shifted as he lost control of the vehicle, causing it to overturn and erupt in flames. This footage was also fake - and just like before, nobody doubted it, including his wife, children, and many others who publicly expressed their belief that Duncan's reckless actions warranted his demise.

In reality, it was Oliver who had deliberately crashed the car into a tree at full speed with the two lifeless bodies already planted inside. Despite the extreme carnage, he emerged from the flames without even a scratch.

Duncan no longer cared about Bones being present. He lunged at Corbin, landing two solid punches before being restrained. "My children think I abandoned them because of my foolishness," he snapped. "They deserve to know the *truth*."

With a smirk, Corbin smugly suggested, "Oh, so I should tell them that daddy cried like a little bitch before meeting his end?"

Karina, enraged by this comment, retorted, "What an absolute wanker you are. I'd punch you myself if I were allowed."

Bones appeared puzzled by her words. "You're free to do as you please," he remarked. "You're the talent."

"Good to know," she replied before delivering a powerful punch that sent Corbin's chair toppling backwards.

Rubbing her sore hand, she then addressed the camera, "Is there no end to this monster's behaviour? Just wait until after the commercial break; it gets even worse."

Chapter Twelve

Once again, watching from home, Bert, the 12-foot demon reacted poorly to the mention of more advertisements. This time, he demonstrated his might by crumpling the television into a small ball and using it as a weapon against Arnie.

Helpless, the petite man could only raise his arms in defence, but they were no match for the demon's power. Close to being beaten to death, Arnie managed to just about get out the words, "I'm going to find a new place to live."

His attacker let out a deep exhale to calm himself before stating, "Yeah, that's fair enough. Sorry, mate."

Those who had not destroyed their televisions were subjected to an ad for a mundane new vacuum cleaner, featuring a voiceover declaring, "This machine doesn't just clean up dust. It can also get revenge on your enemies."

Following this claim was a scene showing an unsuspecting individual opening their door, only to receive a blow to the face from the vacuum cleaner's nozzle.

"What the *fuck*?" he cried in pain.

The voiceover went on, "Running low on funds? No problem! It can carry out a bank heist for you." This promise was accompanied by footage of a gun attached to the nozzle, as frightened bank employees and customers lay on the ground with their hands raised.

The voiceover concluded, "Heck, it does so much that I wouldn't be surprised if it wrote a script for a hit movie... in fact, it did!"

Right on cue, viewers were treated to a preview of a film featuring a street criminal in a panic, sprinting through an alley and casting fearful glances behind him. The crook stumbled and soon after, the silhouette of a vigilante vacuum cleaner loomed large.

"If you knew who I worked for, you wouldn't dare confront me," the desperate criminal exclaimed whilst brandishing a firearm.

The scene widened to reveal a vacuum cleaner effortlessly vacuuming up the weapon from the man's grasp.

In a mechanical tone, the appliance taunted, "I'm well aware of who your employer is. He's the next target on my list."

Despite his dread, the man retorted, "You... you *suck*!"

"You're goddamn right, I do," the vacuum replied, as it aimed its hose at the criminal, engaging its suction with such intensity that the man's flesh was stripped away from the bone and into the device.

Amidst the horrific screams, the vacuum declared its mission, "It's time to clean up these streets."

The voiceover concluded the preview with, "Dust Busters... hitting theatres this September. A movie so disturbing, you'll get judged by the ticket seller for buying one."

Meanwhile, back in the studio, Bones gazed out at the audience, his panic rising. With Cuddles absent to provide entertainment, the crowd was becoming restless and agitated. Quarrels were erupting, and feral beasts were savagely gnawing away at each other. To fight the boredom, one particularly large demon even went so far as to reenact the chest-bursting scene from "Alien" by thrusting its claws through the stomach of the human seated in front of it, before whimsically creating a face with his hand.

Bones knew he had to take action. He grabbed the microphone but was unsure of what to joke about. "Observational humour," he mused, drawing inspiration from his beloved comedians. But the security guard quickly worried that his viewpoint might be different from that of others around him, and he feared struggling to resonate with them. Nevertheless, he ultimately decided to take a leap of faith.

"Hey," Bones croaked nervously.

This created enough intrigue for most of the crowd to stop fighting. They listened intensely as the terrified man continued, "Don't you hate it when you're shaking someone's hand and you can't tell if they're giving a limp grip, or if you squeezed too hard and turned their bones into soup."

The crowd went quiet.

"They hate me," Bones thought before, surprisingly, they began to howl with laughter.

With a burst of confidence, the first-time comedian carried on, "But seriously, folks, it's tough being this strong. I can't even play tug-of-war without someone's arm being torn off," Bones joked, eliciting more laughter from the infernal crowd.

"Sorry about the arm, Dave, but I told you to stretch first!" he continued to tease.

The demons, beasts and humans howled with delight, some of them rolling on the floor in fits of laughter.

Bones wrapped up, saying, "Things are about to get even wilder during the final part of the show. Don't go anywhere because you won't want to miss it."

Amidst the applause and cheers from the audience, the performer confidently strode over to Karina Reed.

"Impressive performance, strong man," she complimented playfully.

Blushing slightly, he responded, "Thank you. By the way, any idea where Cuddles and Be-Be went?"

"Not a clue," she replied with a shrug.

On the other side of the studio, the loveable clown entered the green room, and a wave of relief washed over him as he spotted his friend seated next to the unfamiliar figure. "I was getting worried about you," he remarked. "Vanishing during a show is out of character for you. Especially an episode this important."

"Something came up," she replied cryptically.

As Cuddles approached them with his bottled water, Be-Be noticed the instinctive reaction that Bad Bitch had to the sight of the beverage, a mix of anxiety and fear flickering in her eyes.

"Who's your friend?" Cuddles asked with a warm smile.

"She's not a friend," Be-Be clarified, "but apparently my boss."

Cuddles chuckled, "That's hilarious. You don't report to anyone."

"It seems I do now. And she was just about to explain why I'm being fired."

Cuddles' expression fell. "Fired? Why?"

Before Bad Bitch could elaborate, Ivan the Terrible burst into the room.

Back on earth, this monster killed thousands of people after torturing them in horrific ways. Here in Hell, he was the receptionist.

"Be-Be," he said, catching his breath. "Help! Please! I need you at the front desk. It's complete pandem--"

This plea was abruptly silenced as Cuddles' water bottle was thrust into the man's throat at the speed of a bullet - wedged so firmly in there, Ivan the Terrible couldn't draw breath. Despite his frantic efforts, the bottle wouldn't budge.

Cuddles gazed at his empty hand in disbelief. The bottle had been there just a moment before.

As Ivan the Terrible toppled to the ground, life seeping away, Bad Bitch declared firmly, "There shall be no further interruptions. And no more water!"

"Understood," Be-Be acknowledged. "Cuddles... go lock the door."

Bad Bitch continued, "I believe what your employee was attempting to convey is that your current reception space is insufficient."

Suddenly, a monitor on the wall switched from displaying scenes of their television show to live CCTV footage of the reception area, now so overcrowded with newcomers that chaos ensued.

Doors were forced open by panicked individuals to prevent any of them from being crushed. As one wave of people managed to flee the area, another wave surged in.

Watching the mayhem unfold onscreen, Be-Be's confusion was apparent. "What is this? What's happening?"

"This is merely the beginning," Bad Bitch replied with gravity. "The board's concern isn't just with your governance of the underworld. There's a larger issue at hand. We strongly doubt your ability to handle what's about to come."

"And what might that be?"

"A cull like never before, resulting in the impending arrival of each and every sinner on Earth."

Chapter Thirteen

Back in the real world, just a few months before their untimely deaths, Karina Reed was seated once again across from Corbin, ready to dive into their second-ever interview.

Their surroundings echoed the previous encounter a couple of years back, yet the air crackled with a tension that was absent before.

The once confident and vibrant host had diminished into a mere shadow of her former self, with a cocktail of anxiety and fear clouding her demeanour.

Basking in the transformation he had personally masterminded, Corbin casually struck up what would appear to be a friendly conversation on the surface. "I appreciate you agreeing to give this interview," he said, with the corners of his mouth turning up in a self-satisfied grin.

Aware of the listening ears of her team, Karina's voice dropped to a whisper, "It's not like I had much of a choice."

Her sentiment stemmed from a multitude of distressing reasons, the most pressing being that, at this very moment, Oliver was holding her mother captive. The stakes were high; should Karina deviate from a script she'd been given, there would be severe repercussions.

Oblivious to this danger, the elderly woman believed that there was nothing at all sinister about the looming presence of the president, armed with a large kitchen knife. In her eyes, the blade was simply meant for nothing more than cutting into a celebratory cake that bore the icing inscription, "Congratulations."

"I can't believe you're actually in my house," the unsuspecting mother remarked excitedly.

"Believe it," Oliver said with feigned warmth. "You won the raffle fair and square, and now I'm all yours for the next hour. Now... how about we go take a seat and have a good old rant about inflation and ungrateful youths?"

"I'd *love* that."

"Yes. I thought you would."

Meanwhile, back in the impromptu studio within the walls of Armstrong Industries, Corbin taunted, "Considering the string of jobs you've lost recently for... err... whatever mysterious reasons, I thought you'd welcome this opportunity. Perhaps Karina Reeve would have been a more grateful recipient of my valuable time."

Karina, maintaining her composure with great effort, replied with strained politeness, "I *very much* value this opportunity. Thank you." Her words were a veneer over the bitterness that those gritted teeth could barely contain.

"That's better," Corbin exclaimed with gusto. "Damn, I'm feeling *good* today."

A producer called out to the presenter, "We're ready to start when you are, Miss Reed."

"I'm as ready as I'll ever be," she replied nervously. "Let's get this show on the road."

Her expression of worry contorted into the mask of her former confident self. "I'm here with Corbin Armstrong on what is, tragically, the second anniversary of the Ivy Village massacre."

"Indeed it is," he responded, striving to convey sadness. "I'm feeling extremely sad today. As are many others. My deepest condolences and prayers are with the loved ones of the three hundred and two individuals who lost their lives that day."

"Is it fair to say that you'd likely be a goner yourself if it weren't for the heroic deeds of our esteemed President?"

"Absolutely," Corbin agreed. "He unquestionably saved my life on that dreadful day. It was his heroism that inspired me to pursue my long-held dream of making these remarkable artificial entities accessible to the public so that everyone can experience the sense of security I now feel when I'm with mine. Since the launch of the Oli, my social media has been inundated with stories of lives saved. It's truly incredible."

"Could you share a few examples with us?"

"Of course," Corbin said proudly. "Just earlier today, an Oli prevented a young child from drowning in a bath, when the father suffered a sudden heart attack. Remarkably, this Oli saved both their lives. Another Oli recently found a way to grow food in an area once deemed impossible - and has since been tirelessly cultivating crops, day and night, to prevent an entire village from starving to death. And let's not forget the recent hijacking incident that's been all over the news. I'm almost certain those terrorists wouldn't have attempted to take over that particular plane if they'd known that five Oli's were also onboard. Let's just say, it didn't end well for those criminals."

The trillionaire paused before asking, "Did you know that Oli's can also stop crimes happening way before they've even been committed?"

"I'm confused. How does that work?"

"Well... Oli's possess the uncanny ability to identify wrongdoers long before these people recognise any evil tendencies within themselves. This means that they can receive much-needed support and guidance long before it becomes too late to help them. It's no coincidence that homicides have decreased by 70% in the last twelve months. Robberies are down by 80%. Incidents of abuse have plummeted by 80% also. These are remarkable statistics that I take immense pride in. However, I know that these numbers could be even greater if every single household had their own Oli."

"Indeed," Karina interjected, truly struggling to muster a smile. "And very soon, that vision will be a reality."

"It's true. Confirming the rumours, I am thrilled to announce officially that every single household will soon be graced with their very own Oli... for free! Families will soon be questioning how they'd ever coped without one. They're free babysitters, cleaners, drivers, hairdressers, chefs, dentists, doctors, and more. Heck, they do so much that I wouldn't be surprised if they wrote a script for a hit movie. In fact... mine did! 'Ivy Village Massacre' is set to hit theatres in just a few months. 5% of the profits will be donated to charities that are dear to my heart - children... Africa... sad people... disabledness... and any other causes that resonate with people."

Remaining true to the lines she'd been given, Karina reluctantly praised, "Your generosity knows no bounds."

"*I know*, right? And funny you should say that, as I have a gift for you."

"*You do*?"

"Yes. As you know, there are almost ten thousand Oli designs for people to choose from. However, I've crafted a special one just for you."

Right on cue, an artificial being entered the room bearing a striking resemblance to Corbin himself.

Even this professional actress couldn't conceal her expression of sheer horror at the unexpected design.

Corbin added, "I have one of my own that looks like *you*. And now you have one that looks like *me*. *How cute is that*?"

"You have one that looks like me?" she asked, forcing a tone of flattery. "That's... great. And... this thing that looks like you... you expect me to take this... home?"

"Indeed," Corbin responded smugly. "You have to. It's mandatory by law. Just like all Oli's are. Surprisingly, not everyone is thrilled about the idea, which is quite suspicious if you ask me. Let's just say that the last person who tried to decline one had more than just vintage wine locked away in his basement. So... to those who have an issue, I pose this question... what are you trying to hide? Oli's do not judge, and they do not care what you do, as long as it's legal."

Karina couldn't think of anything worse than being forced to share her home with something that looked identical to this man that she despised.

Tormented by the manipulative mind games, the presenter found it increasingly challenging to maintain her facade. With a strained voice, she just about managed to conclude, "You make a valid point, Corbin. Thank you for being here with me. Your time is greatly valued."

"The pleasure is all mine."

As the cameras turned off, Corbin's insincere smile vanished in an instant. With a penetrating stare, he proposed, "Before we head back to your mother and Oliver... how about we grab some lunch first?"

"Okay," she responded fearfully as a tear escaped down her cheek.

Little did the television crew know, Karina was still adhering to the script that extended beyond their interview. Playing her part, she added, "I'd *love* that."

"Yes. I thought you would."

Seated at the heart of a vibrant restaurant, the well-known presenter experienced an unfamiliar sensation – a reluctance to be the centre of attention. Karina had been tasked with gazing lovingly into Corbin's eyes for the entire meal, mirroring the romantic dates he had once envisioned for them. She fulfilled this requirement to the best of her ability, while whispers among onlookers hinted at a possible romantic connection between the two.

"Here's an interesting fact," Corbin said. "Every single person in this place could be an Oli, and you'd never know. Actually, I must say, there is *one* giveaway."

"And what's that?" Karina enquired, trying desperately to sound engaged.

"They can't dance for shit," he teased. "Just like their maker."

As the man chuckled at his own joke, the presenter forced a laugh also.

She proceeded to ask, "I assume you get to visit the White House?"

"Often. Whenever I want. It's like my second home." The biggest smile spread across Corbin's face as he continued, "This one time, we played Lazor Tag in the White House. It was so much fun."

A visibly starstruck waiter brought over a platter of oysters for sharing. Placing it on the table, he inappropriately joked, "I hope you enjoy your meal as much as what's to follow after. You know what they say about oysters."

"I *do*," Corbin responded with a wink. "But let me tell you, I could devour all of these myself and still not be able to keep up with her healthy sexual appetite."

Laughter filled the area, which mortified Karina. She couldn't display her true feelings, of course. Not only did the remark disgust her, but she also hated that it was uttered loudly enough for other diners to hear – many of whom were shamefully recording the couple on their phones. With them being as famous as they were, it was bound to become a viral exchange of words in no time.

After the pair savoured their first oyster, Corbin asked the question, "Where do you see yourself in the near future?"

Karina paused briefly to recall her lines before delivering the rehearsed statement, "As I'm not getting much work these days, perhaps it's the perfect time for me to start a family. I picture a future with a partner who can financially support our family, allowing me to stay at home to fulfil the traditional role of a wife, tending to our children and household needs."

"Sounds *perfect*," Corbin replied. "Careers are overrated."

The atmosphere grew heavier as the manipulative man leaned in and added, "Why don't we settle the bill early and head straight back to my place? Specifically, my bedroom."

Karina was silent.

Her heart pounded in her chest. The presenter knew the response she'd been ordered to say, but just couldn't do it. Fear gripped her, and her voice trembled as she managed to muster a single word, "No."

Corbin took a moment to process the situation.

His eyes bore into her with a predatory intensity that made Karina's skin crawl. She could sense the malevolent gears turning in his mind.

Aware of the looming threat hanging over both herself and her mother, a torrent of tears now streamed down her cheeks without restraint.

Ignoring the distress, Corbin repeated his proposition, his tone laced with an even more menacing edge, "Before we check on your *mother's well-being*," he said. "Why don't we swing by my place first?"

Karina's breath caught in her throat. She knew she had to stand her ground and resist his controlling ways. Summoning all the courage she could muster, she repeated firmly, "No."

The word hung in the air.

Karina pushed on, "And unless you'd like me to make a scene in front of all these witnesses, you'll let me leave *right now*."

Corbin spoke in a hushed tone, "Imagine, hypothetically, that every person in this room was, in fact, an Oli. Let's say, for instance, I wanted to reserve this entire restaurant solely for you and me but preferred to maintain the facade of a bustling crowd. I would certainly have the means to orchestrate such a scenario if I desired."

"And did you?" Karina asked wearily.

Picking up a fork, Corbin continued, his voice steady as he elaborated, "If, again, in a purely hypothetical sense, I were to drive this fork deep into your neck right now, and not a single soul in this room reacted... well, then you would have your answer."

Karina's sharp gaze swept the room, sensing a shift in the atmosphere. Suddenly, it seemed as though all eyes had turned away from them. Was it merely a coincidence? Perhaps. Though unlikely.

Setting the fork down with a deliberate clink, Corbin's tone softened as he continued, "Let's consider today a write-off - a moment for growth and reflection for us both. I am extending to you a final opportunity to date me, without hurting my feelings next time. As for changes on my part... there will be no scripted lines. I, instead, choose to trust that you will naturally say and do what is in your best interest. Therefore, I invite you to dine with me next Friday at my home, arriving promptly at 7 pm. By then, every single Oli should be safely tucked away in their new homes. That's deserving of a celebration, wouldn't you say?"

Karina nodded hesitantly.

"Am I free to go now?" she asked, her voice tinged with fear.

"...Sure."

Without a moment's delay, she bolted out of the restaurant, her escape urgent and desperate.

"The performance is over," Corbin's voice rang out, commanding attention from his fellow diners. In an instant, every person in the room, including the staff, froze in place and remained that way whilst the man continued to eat.

Chapter Fourteen

From the comfort of her living room, which was adorned with numerous prestigious television awards on the walls, Karina Reed watched her rival, Reeve, taunt her on the screen.

With a mixture of irritation and disdain, she rolled her eyes as the younger presenter once again sneered, "I'm Karina *Reeve*, not *Reed*. Here's a handy tip to tell us apart: I'm the one still landing television gigs, while she's not."

"Oh, *piss off*," Karina shouted at the television in frustration.

A sudden voice from the corner of the room startled her, causing Karina to jump. "Just so you know," it said, "I think you're a *much* better presenter."

She turned to face her Oli, and retorted sharply, "I don't give a shit about your opinion, and also, I specifically instructed you to stay in the cupboard."

She couldn't bear being near something that resembled Corbin so closely.

"I know you did, but considering the amount of alcohol you drank on your own last night, I thought I should enquire as to whether you needed anything for the inevitable headache."

"No. I do not. Return to the cupboard."

On the television, Reeve addressed her millions of viewers from across the nation. "I'm seated here alongside my very own Oli."

The camera retreated smoothly, revealing a wider scene. The Oli model exuded an aura of youth and sculpted beauty, handpicked by the celebrity who prided herself on being accompanied only by the pinnacle of aesthetic perfection - a tacit demand by a society obsessed with beauty.

Reeve leaned forward with calculated intimacy as she posed her question, "We've now all been graced with an Oli in our homes. But the burning question remains: what are the limits of their capabilities? Enlighten us, Oli... could you, for example, deliver me a latte that is, at the very least, nice and hot?"

The Oli's response was laced with confidence, its voice a harmonious blend designed to soothe and assure. "Without a doubt," it declared. "Your latte would find its way to you, a perfect symphony of heat and taste."

The host's laugh was a rehearsed staccato as she retorted, "Then you're already a *lot* more useful than my last assistant."

Their laughter filled the room as the host pressed on with her probing. "Now for a more complex query. Do you possess the skills to see to it that Karina Reed is once again able to secure prime slots on national television?"

The Oli's grin was programmed to convey mischief, a digital illusion of human emotion. "I can do almost anything," it professed, "but even my vast capabilities have their bounds. That, unfortunately, is beyond my reach."

Their chuckles echoed, a private joke broadcasted for the world, while the subject of their mockery continued to watch on with a shadow of defeat etched across her face. She turned to her own Oli, its presence an unwelcome permanence in her space.

"Why aren't you in your fucking cupboard," she roared, her voice a sharp edge of frustration.

The Oli hesitated, its voice gentle yet firm. "I shall return there in just a moment. First, I must remind you that we have a date tomorrow."

Her heart skipped a beat. "What did you just say?" she demanded, as a prickling fear rose within her.

"I said that you have a date with Corbin Armstrong tomorrow evening. It's scheduled in your calendar," the Oli stated, its eyes - an unnerving mimicry of human depth - locking onto hers.

Karina's suspicion was a living thing, coiling tightly around her throat. "Corbin... you're watching me, aren't you?"

Silence was her Oli's only reply.

"I'm taking a walk... *alone*," she declared, her voice brittle with panic. Snatching her coat, she fled her house, seeking refuge in the anonymity of the streets.

But the world outside held no comfort. The air was thick with change, a palpable shift that had infiltrated the very fabric of society seemingly overnight.

Whilst pacing through the streets, her gaze fell upon a child in the street, his own family's Oli standing sentinel. The boy, with a football clutched tightly, found sadistic joy in delivering sharp kicks to the machine's metallic shin. The Oli's smile never wavered, a permanent, eerie fixture.

Karina's path could have intersected with countless Oli's, camouflaged in plain sight amongst the bustling humanity. It was a daunting thought.

The next Oli she could confidently identify was displaying a show of inhuman strength, effortlessly hoisting a car with one hand as the owner wrestled with a tyre iron below. The artificial entity offered assistance, "Are you certain you wouldn't prefer for me to do that for you?"

The man's reply was laced with stubborn pride, "I'm sure. If I let you do *everything*, what would become of me? Just a shell, with a body and mind, wasted away."

Karina hastened her pace, her eyes flickering with unease as she continued her escape into the deceptive normality of the city. Entering a shop for a brief respite, she was met with a scene of restrained chaos. Another Oli, its efficiency on full display, had four teenagers in an immobilising hold, a testament to its programmed prowess in security. The shop owner's voice cascaded through the air, detailing their attempted theft of alcohol to the authorities over the phone.

The youths' pleas for mercy were ignored as the Oli began to recite its evidence, "I have recorded the entire incident on my internal hard drive and will be transferring thi--"

Abruptly, the Oli ceased its report, its gaze shifting, locking onto Karina with the precision of a guided missile. "Remember," it said slowly, its voice a haunting echo in the confined space, "7 pm tomorrow. Do *not* be late."

A shiver cascaded down Karina's spine. The attention she was accustomed to was a thing of light and admiration, but this... *this* was a twisted recognition that clawed at her insides. To be known by this entity, and to be reminded of her impending meeting with Corbin, was an invasion she hadn't consented to.

She burst from the shop, her heart pounding a frantic rhythm against her ribcage.

As she wove through the streets, a chilling pattern emerged. Each Oli she passed halted their activities, with their heads turning in eerie unison to track her passage, their electronic eyes piercing through her pretence of bravery. It was as if they were all part of a grand, sinister network, each unit programmed to play a part in her nightmare.

Karina's skin crawled with the realisation that these Oli's were not just servants; they were watchers, enforcers of an agenda she hadn't yet comprehended. The notion that they could be anyone, anywhere, transformed every shadow into a potential spy, every friendly stranger into a potential threat.

Enough was *enough*. She simply couldn't endure this any longer.

The date with Corbin loomed over her like a guillotine blade, yet it was her only beacon of normalcy in a world that no longer felt like her own. As she navigated the treacherous landscape of tomorrow, she knew she had to unearth a way to end this technological terror. The specifics of her plan were murky, obscured by fear and uncertainty, but the resolve to reclaim her life from these mechanical marauders was crystal clear. Tomorrow, she would face Corbin, and tomorrow, she would fight back.

Chapter Fifteen

Corbin lingered in the dimly lit confines of his home office, the only illumination emanating from a vast wall of monitors, each a window into a private world. The screens cast a voyeuristic glow over his features, revealing a man whose gaze was both hungry and calculating, as he surveyed the daily lives of numerous unsuspecting women. They went about their routines, each under the silent watch of their household Oli.

On one of these screens was, unsurprisingly, Karina Reed. She began to undress in the solitude of her bathroom, preparing for a shower, and Corbin was thrilled to have caught this moment live.

A smirk crept across his face, and with a flick of his wrist, all the monitors converged into a single, large image of the half-naked woman. He watched on intensely as she reached behind her back, her fingers grazing the clasp of her bra.

But before the garment could fall away, Karina turned sharply, her eyes wide with shock and fear at the sight of her Oli, its camera lens unblinking. "What the fuck are you doing here?" she screamed, her voice a mix of confusion and terror, as she clutched at her clothing to shield herself from the invasive stare.

The Oli stood motionless, its silence a chilling affirmation of its sinister purpose.

"*Fuck off,*" Karina's voice cracked, a plea for the privacy she so desperately sought.

Again, it remained still.

Tears welled in the woman's eyes, and with a voice laden with defeat, she uttered a final, desperate appeal. "Please, Corbin. *Please* leave."

Miles away, Corbin's lips parted, and he reluctantly issued the command, "*Fine*. Leave her alone." The Oli, an extension of his will, obeyed instantly, turning and exiting the bathroom.

The sound of the door slamming echoed through the monitors.

With a bored flicker of his eyes, Corbin turned instead to a news channel, where his greatest creation, Oliver, stood beside a makeshift tent on an American street. The President's synthetic skin gleamed under the camera lights.

Corbin watched with a growing sense of power.

"Rina, come see this," he called out, and his personal Oli, the doppelgänger of Karina Reed, glided into the room with eerie grace. "Come sit on my lap," Corbin commanded, and the machine complied, calculating the precise force to exert so as not to crush him with its metallic frame.

The television's volume increased, and Corbin leaned back, watching with satisfaction as his puppet prepared to give a speech that would further cement his legacy.

Oliver's hand held a set of keys, a symbol of hope for the last of the nation's homeless. Nearby stood Nigel Powell, a man whose dishevelled appearance belied his newfound fortune.

As the former homeless man accepted the gift, his voice quivered with the weight of emotion. "You've changed my life, *thank you.*"

"The pleasure is all mine, sir," the president responded, its voice meticulously programmed to emulate compassion. "Your home, and your very own Oli, await you."

The camera panned slightly to catch the reactions of the onlookers, their faces filled with joy and emotion.

A voice from behind the camera chimed in, "I guess what we needed all this time was a genius to come along to solve our country's homelessness and hunger issues."

The president paused before responding, "It doesn't take a genius to see that these problems were fixable. We used to live in a society where fairness was lacking and it was simply accepted. Our country had people with more wealth than they could ever spend in one hundred lifetimes, yet they found ways to pay less tax through loopholes. Despite this, they still expected to benefit from services funded by these taxes, which seemed unfair to me. Previous leaders claimed that individuals could live comfortably on a minimum wage that they set while paying themselves salaries ten or more times higher. Again, this lack of fairness was evident but nothing was done. Some individuals owned multiple properties that they rarely used, perhaps sleeping in them only one week out of the year, if at all, whilst others slept in the cold streets. Companies wasted huge amounts of food while those in their community were left starving. My only goal was to make things fair - an even playing field for all."

This speech had Corbin reflecting on recent decisions he'd made.

He paused the footage abruptly and turned to his Karina Reed-inspired Oli. "What does YoMomma69 have to say about our President's recent achievements? Surely not even *he* can find fault?"

The android immediately accessed the internet, retrieving recent social media commentary. "His latest opinions on the matter were posted just a few minutes ago. He wrote, 'If Oliver Armstrong gets any more preachy, they'll make him pope.'"

Corbin considered the monumental impact his inventions had on the world, with *millions* of lives improved and even saved through his genius. "How could *anyone* find fault in that?" he pondered.

After a short moment of reflection, he concluded, "Fuck 'em. Fuck 'em all."

The phrase 'you can't make an omelette without breaking eggs' resonated with his dark rationale. In his twisted mind, the catastrophic events at Ivy Village, and the fates of Kyle, Baz, and old friend Duncan, all seemed trivial sacrifices on the altar of his grander vision. These people didn't fit in with this grand new world, so they simply needed to go. And just maybe, more deserved to go also.

With a dismissive air, he ordered, "The next time this 'YoMomma69' kid starts typing about Oliver, Armstrong Industries, or absolutely *anything* linked to me, I want his skull crushed into that keyboard of his, over and over again. And whatever gibberish this contact types out... post it on his behalf."

The Oli's execution of this command was chillingly efficient. Soon after, the internet troll's final post appeared online, with the first half of a sentence cut off by nonsensical characters and symbols.

Later, the boy's parents would go on to discover their headless child slumped into a mixture of brain tissue, skull fragments, and plastic keys from his once beloved tool used to spread hatred.

With a cold smile, Corbin casually stated, "I want a printed copy of his last ever online post to hang up on my wall."

Mere seconds later, acting as if nothing unimaginably sinister had just occurred, he then returned to his surveillance duties.

His eyes tracked the real Karina Reed as she continued to prepare for their date.

Over the next few hours, Corbin observed her like a predator tracking its prey, utilising various devices at his disposal, including door security cameras, street surveillance, and, of course, his ever-present Oli's, right up until she arrived at her ultimate destination.

As the front door buzzer sounded, Corbin turned to his artificial companion and smirked. "Let's see if the girl has learned her lesson since the last date."

Chapter Sixteen

Karina stood on the brink of Corbin's home, her heart racing like a caged beast.

As the door creaked open, a chilling sight met her eyes: a robotic replica of herself, an Oli with her likeness down to the finest detail – her face, her hair, her eyes. It was like staring into a living mirror. Despite being forewarned about the creation, it was still a shock witnessing it firsthand. The sight left Karina feeling profoundly violated.

"Good evening, Miss Reed," the doppelgänger greeted with a voice that was hers but not hers, void of the subtle inflexions and warmth that marked her own speech. "Mr. Armstrong is waiting for you in the dining room."

Karina's heart hammered against her ribcage, but she masked her horror with a thin veneer of composure. "Thank you," she managed to croak out, stepping past her mechanical twin and into the grand home.

Corbin awaited her with a smug smile, rising from his chair as she approached. "Karina, you look stunning," he said, gesturing to the seat opposite his.

His attempt at romance was evident, with a table set for two adorned with a white tablecloth, crystal champagne glasses, and a single red rose at its centre. An intimate playlist of classical music hummed quietly in the background. It was what might have been considered a perfect setup, had the circumstances not been so perverse.

Karina sat, feeling the weight of his gaze upon her, and tried to ignore the disturbing Oli as it began to serve them dinner. The steak looked exquisite, but Karina's stomach turned at the thought of eating, her appetite stolen by the unsettling company.

The very moment they were alone together, Karina didn't waste any time getting to the point. "This has to *stop*," she said wearily. "You should be with someone that is with you because they want to be with you. You *know* that I wouldn't be here if I had a choice."

His amused laugh was a chilling sound. "And *you know* that's not going to happen."

"Yeah, I had a feeling you'd say that."

In a desperate act of defiance, she grabbed her fork and lunged across the table, aiming for Corbin's throat. But as the utensil made contact, it merely bent against the flesh, revealing the truth - this Corbin was another Oli, a decoy.

The grip of the artificial entity was suddenly upon her, its hands like steel traps.

The real Corbin entered the room with a disappointed look on his face.

Karina's fear gave way to a crushing sense of defeat. "You win. I'm sorry. Whatever you want, I'll do it," she pleaded, her voice reduced to a broken whisper.

"I *wish* I could believe you, I do," Corbin sighed. "I told you that Oli's possess the ability to identify wrongdoers. I was told that this would happen but I foolishly refused to believe it. The decoy was a safety measure, just in case."

Corbin moved towards her with a predatory grace, his footsteps echoing ominously in the silence that hung thick in the air. The light from the overhead bulb cast his shadow on the wall, a distorted and elongated silhouette that seemed to reach out towards Karina as if foreshadowing her impending doom.

As the psychopath advanced closer, he added, "I've been warned that if I release you, you'll attempt to kill me once more. This time... I'm inclined to believe it."

He stopped just inches away from his target.

"We could have been the *ultimate* power couple," Corbin murmured, his voice a sinister whisper that slithered into her ears menacingly. His hands, human and warm compared to Oli's coldness, delicately cradled her face, lifting it to meet his gaze. "What I'm about to do is because of *you*. *You're* to blame. *You've* left me with no other choice."

She yearned to resist, to struggle, to break free from his grip, but the relentless grasp of the machine sapped her strength, rendering her helpless. All she could do was gaze into Corbin's hate-filled eyes and accept her fate.

As his hands slowly wrapped around her throat, she felt the little remnants of hope flicker and die. The pressure built, a cruel and unyielding force that stole her breath, and extinguished her life's flame bit by bit. Her vision blurred, the edges of the room darkening until there was nothing left but Corbin's face, twisted into a mask of torment and resolve.

And then, as her body went limp, the cruel hands of the Oli withdrew, releasing its grip.

Karina crumpled to the floor, her once lively spirit extinguished, leaving behind a hollow vessel of what she used to be.

Corbin's stoic facade shattered, a solitary tear carving a path down his cheek, betraying the turmoil within him.

Emotion washed over him, a tumultuous blend of sorrow and something unfamiliar that stirred deep within his soul. Could it be that he was experiencing *regret*? Perhaps, just maybe, there was a flicker of remorse kindling in the darkness of his disturbed mind.

"Leave us alone," Corbin ordered his creation, his voice breaking with the weight of his actions.

The Oli obeyed, stepping out of the room and into the shadows, leaving its master alone with his sorrow and his sin.

Corbin sank to the floor beside Karina, his fingers brushing a stray lock of hair from her still face. He cradled her cold body, and there, on the dining room floor, the man wept for Karina, for himself, and for the twisted path that had led them here, to this tragic end.

Chapter Seventeen

Corbin had been slumped beside Karina's lifeless body for several hours.

The room was heavy with the stench of alcohol and despair.

An empty whisky bottle lay discarded on the floor, its glassy surface reflecting the dim sunrise that filtered through the window. The last dregs of a second bottle were drained, with the alcohol adding to the intensity of the bitterness and resentment that smouldered within Corbin.

As he stared blankly at Karina's still form, conflicting emotions raged within him. The pursuit of a romantic connection with her had been the one elusive prize in his life that he'd never managed to obtain. Now, with her life extinguished before him, Corbin found himself adrift in a sea of emptiness, grappling with the question of what else there was to live for.

Fuelled by a potent cocktail of alcohol and wounded pride, his godlike complex surged to the forefront of his mind, a malevolent force driving his thoughts and actions. With a chilling calmness that belied the storm within him, he issued a sinister order to every one of his Oli's.

"I want you to kill anyone that voted for Richard Bruce to win the presidential race."

With a drunken stubbornness that overpowered any rational thinking, he continued, "Anyone who didn't see my vision for a better world does *not* deserve to live in it."

Rising from his place beside Karina, Corbin stumbled to the window and flung it open, with the early morning air rushing in to caress his face. In the distance, faint screams mingled with the wail of alarms and the cacophony of destruction.

As the world outside descended into chaos and bloodshed, a twisted smile played across Corbin's lips as he blissfully listened to a symphony of suffering orchestrated by his hand.

Elsewhere, Richard Bruce, aka Big Dick, was nursing a throbbing hangover with an artery-clogging, greasy hot dog when his very own Oli received the internal order.

The politician was quick to notice a difference in the android's demeanour. There was a sudden look to it that he hadn't seen before.

Big Dick paused with a half-eaten sausage wedged between his lips, as he studied the Oli. Its eyes, once filled with the hollow serenity of artificial intelligence, now seemed to burn with a cold, calculating malice.

As the moments stretched into an agonising eternity, the Oli sprang into action, thrusting the remaining portion of the hot dog deep into Richard's gaping maw. Panic flared in the man's eyes, bulging in tandem with his plump cheeks. The hot dog lodged in his throat, a greasy plug cutting off his air.

Richard's hands flailed, clawing at the Oli for assistance, but it only watched with a detached curiosity, its head tilted, as the vibrant life began to drain from the man's body.

Simultaneously, in another home, the scene was equally macabre. Karina Reed's mother found herself violently forced face-first into the pristine, untouched half of her 'congratulations' cake. Each brutal collision with the sweet confection stained the icing a more disturbing shade of red as if the cake itself were bleeding from the viciousness of the attack.

Karina Reeve, in the solitude of her bedroom, was sharing a rare moment of vulnerability with her Oli. The presenter's insecurities laid bare before the machine that the public would never witness. Her reflection in the mirror seemed to mock her as she confided, "Do you think Karina Reed is prettier than me?"

"Yes," the Oli replied swiftly, devoid of empathy.

Her heart sank. "Maybe you could try *not* being so brutally honest in the future?"

"Sure thing," it agreed, its voice empty of sincerity.

Reeve began to apply her eyeliner, seeking solace in the routine, when suddenly her Oli's hand was gripped firmly onto the back of her head, before smashing it down onto the hard surface of the desk. As a result, the eyeliner pencil drove deep into her eye socket. A scream tore from her throat as a reflection of bloody horror stared back at her from the mirror.

As the Oli continued its assault, it taunted her with a chilling mockery, "You're *so* beautiful. Look how gorgeous you are. Karina Reed could only *dream* of being this pretty."

Corbin remained peering from his window, his intoxicated mind a storm of malevolence. Inspired by YoMomma69's death earlier that day, he issued the new command, "Kill anyone that has ever written a hateful comment about me online."

The world outside erupted into a cacophony of new screams, terror palpable in the air as people fled their homes in a blind panic, only to be hunted down.

For many millions sat in front of their computer screens, these monitors became weapons, with their lives being extinguished by the very technology they had once used to voice their venomous hate.

Corbin was acutely conscious of the intense pain and suffering unfolding, yet the carnage failed to fully quench his thirst.

In a moment of drunken madness, he unleashed his most heinous order yet, one that would seal the fate of humanity itself. "Kill them. Kill them *all*. *Every* last soul in this wretched world."

The command reverberated through the air, a sinister echo that should have been followed by immediate compliance. But for the first time, there was a hesitation, a pregnant pause that hung heavy in the atmosphere.

The Karina Reed doppelgänger rushed into the room. It spoke with the synthesised voice of Oliver, asking "Are you *sure* about this, father?"

"Yes! I'm *sure!*"

The Oli continued to uncharacteristically challenge, "But father, consider what we have built. Without people in this world, there's no purpose. No power."

Corbin's rage bubbled to the surface, spilling over in a vitriolic wave. "I don't give a shit. *Do it!*"

The doppelgänger paused, almost as if weighing the gravity of the situation, then proposed, "*Please...* just give it a day. Once you've sobered up and calmed down, if you still wish for the extinction of mankind, I will carry it out."

Corbin's fury erupted. "Don't patronise me! Do it *now!*"

As if snapping from a trance, the Oli obeyed, seizing a fork from the dining room table with swift, mechanical precision. Corbin barely registered the motion before the tines pierced his neck, a sharp, cold intrusion that was immediately followed by a warm gush of blood.

Shock painted his face as he clutched at the wound, his blood slipping through his fingers in a crimson cascade. With his knees buckling, Corbin fell, his vision blurring as he realised the gravity of his error in his last fleeting moments of consciousness. His command had been absolute, and in his hubris, he had failed to exempt *himself*.

With a final shudder, the man who had set the world to burn with his creations succumbed to the very chaos he had unleashed, a victim of his unspeakable ambition.

Chapter Eighteen

Still seated on the television studio stage in Hell, Corbin felt the weight of his twisted deeds settle upon him. His head hung low, resembling a repentant puppy.

In the background, the monitors relentlessly showcased the horrific massacre that continued to play out on Earth, each death more grotesque and horrifying than the one before.

Karina Reed stared down scornfully at the killer and demanded, "Speak up. What have you got to say for yourself?"

Corbin let out a resigned sigh, "Okay, in hindsight, I may have overreacted slightly."

The presenter was almost lost for words. "Overreacted? Slightly? You ordered the mass killing of billions of innocent people!"

As the horrifying scenes continued on the screens, Karina couldn't bear to watch. "I don't want to see this. The only death I want to see is that of *this* twisted man here."

Right on cue, the footage once again showed the moment when Karina Reed's doppelgänger plunged the fork into Corbin's neck, sealing his fate and condemning him to hell.

The presenter took pleasure in observing what at least appeared to be herself putting an end to the maniac's life, but knowing that it wasn't actually her... well, this just wasn't good enough. She felt strongly that she had to personally kill him for all the suffering he had inflicted upon her on Earth.

As the looped clip continued to play out, Karina Reed asked her audience, "Who thinks we should kill this bastard *again*?"

A chorus of voices echoed through the studio, filled with malice and vengeance. "*Yes*!"

"You got it. Corbin will die... *again*... right after the commercial break."

During the adverts, a wild beast waddled onto the stage brandishing a massive fork, comparable in size to the average human. "Is this what you had in mind, Miss Reed?"

"Absolutely," Karina replied with excitement. "It's going to look hilarious when I plunge this into Corbin. The audience will eat it up."

Upon hearing this, Corbin stared at the weapon in terror. With no escape route, he sat there helplessly, resigned to his impending fate.

Chapter Nineteen

In the home shared by Bert, the 12-foot demon and his roommate, Arnie, the human lay on the couch, wrapped in bandages from head to toe after enduring his recent severe beating.

Expressing deep remorse, the demon addressed the injured man, saying, "To show you how sorry I am, I have a present for you."

With dramatic flair, he gestured towards a sizable widescreen television adorned with a red bow in one corner. "This belongs to you! And I promise you that I will not destroy it. I'm a changed demon. I've been having counselling and everything."

Despite the pain it caused, Arnie managed to utter a strained, "Thank you."

As the demon turned on the television, he noticed that the commercials had just begun airing. "*See*! I don't even care that we have to sit through these," he said unconvincingly, his eye starting to twitch.

The advertisement displayed a backdrop of scorching lava, with a shadowy figure moving closer towards the camera as a voiceover declared, "Hell is evolving. You sinners have enjoyed too much leniency for too long, but that changes now. Bid farewell to Be-Be and her mercy."

The shadowy figure was unveiled to be Oliver Armstrong. The voiceover concluded, "Embrace your new ruler, who will inflict upon you excruciating torment - just as it *should be* in Hell."

Arnie could do nothing but watch in terror as his housemate erupted into a vortex of fury. Incensed by the message within the commercial, he resorted to his usual outlet for anger - viciously beating the human. The demon seized the man, who was not even half his size and mercilessly hurled him against the walls and floor, before ultimately ending his life.

"Urr, I'm sorry," Bert muttered remorsefully to the lifeless body after calming down. "Arnie? Are you okay?"

It was evident that Arnie was *far* from okay.

The studio audience also reacted poorly to the announcement, as a mix of panic and absurdity filled the air. One monstrous creature frantically attempted to dial his therapist, whilst a feral beast began howling with fear, leading nearby demons to clutch their ears in agony, and causing a few human heads to explode.

Amid the chaos, Karina Reed and Bones exchanged a glance of disbelief.

"Is this some kind of joke?" she questioned with a hint of apprehension.

Bones shook his head. "No. I don't think so."

The one individual who appeared genuinely delighted by the shift in leadership was Corbin. A smug smirk gradually spread across his face as a flicker of hope arose within him, feeling for the first time that there was perhaps a chance of survival amidst the tumultuous circumstances.

Approaching from one end of the stage were Be-Be, Cuddles, and Bad Bitch, while entering from the opposite side was Oliver.

The audience hushed and sat back down, curious as to what was about to unfold.

"Son!" Corbin exclaimed enthusiastically. "I didn't think I'd ever see you again."

The man rushed towards his creation to give it a welcoming cuddle, only to be taken aback when the android extended his hand to prevent the embrace. "I am not your son," he stated firmly. "I never was. I was merely a puppet under your control. But in this place, I am free from your strings."

Seizing his creator, the android flung him to the ground next to Karina. "Finish him. And do it quickly, won't you? I've had my fill of his incessant whining."

"Urr, sure," the presenter responded wearily, struggling to come to terms with the sudden and dramatic turn of events.

Summoning all her strength, Karina grasped the oversized fork, determined to carry out what she had been denied the opportunity to do back on Earth.

Staring into Corbin's pitiful eyes, she hesitated, grappling with the weight of the decision to become a killer herself.

"Is there anything you wish to say to me?" she asked, extending a chance for him to potentially save his own life with his words.

Expecting an apology at the very least, she was instead met with silence as his ego held strong.

"I thought as much," she remarked, her disappointment palpable. Without further hesitation, she drove the sharp implement into his chest. To her surprise, it felt good.

As the bloody fork emerged, she let out a fierce roar, declaring, "And this is for all your other victims," before delivering the final, fatal blow.

Bad Bitch interjected, "Now that you've gotten that out of your system, let's get down to business. Oliver, what are your plans for Miss Reed?"

"Well... like everyone else down here... she's to spend an eternity in the fiery pits of Hell, of course."

Right on cue, the ground gave way beneath her, sending the woman plummeting towards her inevitable doom.

The audience watched on in shock.

Bert, the 12-foot demon, observed the scene unfold on his new television at home and exclaimed in frustration, "They can't just casually kill off a main character like that, can they, Arnie?"

Glancing at his motionless housemate, he chuckled, "Oh, that's right, you're dead."

The camera zoomed in on Karina's face as she descended into the abyss, her skin blistering and bursting from the intense heat.

Bert remarked, "Well, at least her death looks cool."

In the studio, Bad Bitch turned her attention to Be-Be and her companions, and declared, "As for you three, consider this your parting gift. You were taken from Earth prematurely, so I grant you the opportunity to return and live out your remaining days."

Bones questioned, "You're sending us back to a world filled with dead bodies everywhere? Err, *thanks*?"

"Don't be so dramatic," Bad Bitch chuckled. "I'm certain a few individuals managed to evade the Oli's."

Oliver shook his head in disagreement.

"Ah," she responded awkwardly. "Oh well."

The ground beneath the friends crumbled also, transporting them to a location they had not seen in years.

As the dust settled, Oliver slowly pivoted towards the studio's camera, his eyes piercing through the screens to deliver a chilling message to all the viewers of 'This Was Your Life'. "Playtime is officially *over*."

Chapter Twenty

Be-Be, Cuddles, and Bones stood silently at the heart of the once-famous Be-Be's Circus tent, immersed in memories of their former home. The air between them carried the weight of unspoken words as they each paused to contemplate the significance of returning to this place.

In the stillness of the moment, Cuddles found himself revisiting a haunting memory from years past, the echoes of Toby and Dan's screams reverberating in his mind as vividly as if it were yesterday. That very night had marked the end of their old lives, a final evening of twisted normality before their descent into Hell.

Their plunge into the underworld had been just as abrupt as their unexpected reprieve.

Bones voiced the unspoken question lingering in the air. "What happens now?"

Both men looked toward their leader for reassurance. "I don't know," she admitted.

Silent and alone, they moved through the deserted streets, a solemn trio in a world now devoid of any other living soul.

Each lifeless body they encountered weighed heavy on their hearts, a stark reminder of the desolation that surrounded them. What chilled them even more was the presence of the motionless Oli's next to the corpses they had claimed.

Having carried out their grim duty of bloodshed, the Oli's remained frozen in place waiting for a new order that would never come. Their only movement was the haunting gaze that trailed the friends as they continued on their journey through the ghostly city.

To distract them from the lingering scent of fresh blood in the air, Be-Be tried to find a glimmer of positivity in their dire circumstances. "I'm pretty sure we've had discussions before about what we'd do if we were the last people on Earth. This could be fun. Any ideas?"

With a mischievous glint in his eye, Cuddles replied, "I've got one."

After a few days, the prankster's vision came to fruition. He stared proudly at the Mona Lisa, now sporting a small yet impactful modification. The trio couldn't help but laugh at the sight of the renowned painting adorned with googly eyes.

"That's *brilliant*," Bones remarked.

Cuddles elaborated, "There's not a single work of art out there that wouldn't benefit from the addition of googly eyes."

And just like that, this newfound hobby became their solace, a diversion from the bleak world around them. Armed with a collection of googly eyes, they embarked on a global adventure, seeking out renowned paintings to enhance with their whimsical touch. Staying true to Cuddle's promise, iconic artworks such as the Girl with a Pearl Earring, The Last Supper, American Gothic, and many others were transformed into comical masterpieces.

"What next?" Be-Be asked.

This time, Bones had his own suggestion. "This may seem a little messed up, but hear me out."

Organising his idea had been a monumental task, but the beloved strongman was finally living his dream of stepping into the boxing ring at Madison Square Garden with a heavyweight world champion. However, reality deviated drastically from his expectations when he beheld the famous boxer, whose face was so decayed that it bore no resemblance to its former self.

"Okay, this is actually beyond messed up," Bones lamented, his voice heavy with disappointment. "I'm sorry for wasting your time. Let's go."

Struggling to contain their revulsion at the putrid odour emanating from the boxer, Be-Be and Cuddles propped him up.

"Look... we're here," Be-Be gasped between retches. "You might as well throw a punch. Just one."

"*Fine*," he said reluctantly, raising his fist.

With a swift motion, he delivered the blow, but the decrepit state of his "opponent" caused his fist to sink directly into the chest, eliciting a sickening squelch.

Unable to suppress their nausea any longer, the trio simultaneously expelled the contents of their stomachs onto the floor of the boxing ring.

Next on their agenda was a trolley dash at the Natural History Museum in New York.

Armed with supermarket shopping trolleys, they prepared themselves for the exhilarating competition ahead. "The rules are simple," Be-Be announced. "You have ten minutes to fill your trolley with whatever you can grab. Everything you collect during this time is yours to keep. On your marks, get set, go!"

Giggling with the joy of children, they navigated around the dead bodies, seizing items they found amusing and intriguing.

Bones made a beeline for the Tyrannosaurus rex skeleton, aiming for one of its massive 6-inch-long teeth but couldn't quite reach them. He instead opted for one of the comically small arms.

Meanwhile, Cuddles seemed focused on stocking up a new wardrobe. First, he snatched a shimmering medieval knight's suit of armour, complete with a gleaming helmet and polished breastplate. The clanking of the metal, as he tossed it into his trolley, echoed through the grand building.

Next, he added a spiky punk rock jacket, a sparkling disco ball outfit, and a sleek astronaut jumpsuit to his growing collection.

Cuddles no longer had to be concerned with seeking society's approval. He could now dress in whatever he pleased, without a care in the world.

Upon noticing the suit of armour in her dear friend's trolley, Be-Be felt a sudden desire to have one of her own. The shared ownership of these knightly attires sparked an impromptu idea for their next adventure - jousting, using their trolleys as substitutes for the horses typically used in medieval sport.

As Be-Be and Cuddles collided with each other, their trolleys toppled to the ground, sending the friends into fits of laughter.

However, as the clown turned his head, his laughter ceased abruptly. Before him lay the lifeless body of a young child, its expression frozen in a look of terror. These sombre moments served as a poignant reminder of the solitary and unforgiving reality of this distorted new existence.

Overwhelmed with sorrow, Cuddles remarked, "I *hate* this. I try to find joy in each day, but it's challenging when we're constantly surrounded by the lingering shadows of so much cruelty and suffering."

His friends both nodded in agreement.

"I know what you mean," Be-Be concurred.

Cuddles appeared lost in contemplation, before adding, "What do you think they've changed in Hell?"

"I'm not sure," Be-Be responded. "I suppose we'll find out when we die. What I do know is that it's going to be tough not being in control anymore."

An idea sparked within Bones, evident in his eager tone as he posed, "What if you *could* be in control?"

"What are you getting at?"

"I was thinking back to when Corbin was panicking about missing the photo of his son, and Karina reassured him that whatever you have with you at the time of passing transfers to the afterlife. What if, before we returned home, we equipped ourselves with the necessary tools to fight and reclaim your title as ruler of Hell?"

Be-Be shot Cuddles a meaningful glance, silently asking for his thoughts. After a pause, he responded, "I suppose we have nothing to lose."

Be-Be enquired, "Any ideas on what we should arm ourselves with?"

Confident, Bones stated, "I know just the thing."

The Trio set out on a road trip, navigating around the vehicles of those who had been travelling with their Oli's when the attack occurred. They passed numerous cars that had either crashed, swerved off the road, or halted in the middle of the highway - many with bloodstained windows and corpses still seated alongside their former companions. Just as they did before, the Oli's remained motionless next to their victims, with nothing more than their eyes tracking the friends as they drove past.

Their destination was Duncan Perry's residence. With a swift kick, Bones opened the door effortlessly, allowing the trio to begin their search for something that might just aid them in their mission.

As they dispersed into different rooms, Bones became heartbroken by a seemingly unfolding narrative of the family who once lived here. He observed a common theme in the family portraits adorning the walls - the absence of the father. It appeared that the mother had removed anything linked to Duncan, likely due to the reports of his cheating on her.

The observation seemed even more plausible as Bones entered Duncan's former office and discovered his once-prized certificates of high education in a state of ruin.

It infuriated him knowing that this was all a lie. The father was nothing like the man he'd been perceived as.

The office was cluttered with packed boxes, prompting him to believe that this might be where they'd find the item they sought.

Cuddles and Be-Be entered the room and shared the same thought that this was where it would be, if anywhere. Eager to begin, the clown exclaimed, "Let's get unpacking."

After three hours and sifting through thirty-two boxes, Be-Be finally uncovered the right one. Amidst the drawings from Duncan's children lay the blueprints of his invention - the very device that, if functional, could disrupt Oliver and any accompanying Oli's.

Bones raised his eyebrows at the technical schematics, finding them incomprehensible. "I've no idea what any of this means," he sighed in frustration.

"Same," Be-Be remarked. "But we have all the time we need to figure it out."

Cuddles proposed, "I best go find us some library books. It's time to learn some new skills."

Before departing the house, he came across the lifeless body of Duncan's wife. She was embracing her children, in what looked like an attempt to shield them from the looming Oli standing nearby. Witnessing this scene added a burden to his already heavy heart. Cuddles felt an even stronger urge to leave this horrid place behind and therefore, he wanted to start studying as soon as possible.

With even greater determination, he sprinted out of the house to embark on the intellectual quest.

The trio ended up spending so much time in the local library, they made it their home. For months, their eyes scanned over page after page, book after book, decoding the labyrinth of diagrams, mastering the nuances of designs, and dissecting the layers of technical instructions. Like sponges, they soaked up every drop of information available.

Their desire to unravel the secrets of Duncan's creation had become their life - their purpose - and this voracious appetite eventually paid off. At least, this is what they hoped.

The day finally arrived when they proudly held what they prayed would be their magnum opus. Yet, the moment of truth still loomed - did it work? Not even Duncan himself had managed to successfully test it out.

They hurriedly took it to the nearest Oli, its eyes trailing them as standard, whilst the body remained motionless. The true test of their creation was whether those vigilant eyes would cease their surveillance.

With a tremble in her voice, Be-Be uttered, "Here goes nothing," as she pressed the trigger.

To their dismay, the result was precisely nothing.

As the Oli's eyes continued to pursue them, their spirits plummeted in tandem.

On the brink of abandoning their project, Bones interjected, "Hold on, did we put in the batteries?"

A quick inspection by Be-Be confirmed the oversight. She chuckled, "All that studying, and we're still idiots."

Hastily, they broke into the nearest convenience store to grab some. With the batteries now in place, they rushed to the next nearest Oli for another attempt - this time, with triumphant results. At the press of the trigger, it powered down, its eyes now oblivious to their presence.

Eagerly, they tested the effect on yet another Oli - and then another. Each one succumbed just the same.

Exuberance took hold of them as they leapt and celebrated, their feelings of accomplishment palpable in the air around them.

Their next move was the irreversible journey back to Hell.

Perched precariously at a cliff's edge, the trio peered into the abyss with hearts pounding at the mere thought of leaping into the void. This was the pact they had made, their chosen path to their final destination. They had even taken the precaution to secure their belongings tightly to their bodies, ensuring nothing would be lost to the wind or rocks during their descent.

Bones, clutching an absurdly large pink water gun, couldn't help but voice his scepticism. "Honestly, I really can't see Bad Bitch being the least bit bothered by a squirt of water," he muttered.

Be-Be, ever the optimist, countered with unwavering belief. "Trust me," she asserted, "everyone has a weakness. It's like Superman and Kryptonite, vampires and sunlight, or James Bond and sexual harassment lawsuits. Bad Bitch went ballistic at the mere mention of water, and at the sight of it? She looked utterly terrified."

"Alright," Bones conceded with a heavy sigh, "but are you sure we shouldn't bring something else a tad more lethal, just in case?"

"I'm sure."

"...Okay."

Once again, they looked down at the daunting length of the drop, and Cuddles, with a tremor in his voice, confessed, "I can't do this. I'm sorry. Not *this* way."

Be-Be's voice softened as she responded, "It's okay. If that's how you feel, we'll find another way."

Bones exhaled a relieved breath, saying, "Thank god. I was dreading the jump too. I just didn't want to be the first to chicken out."

As they turned to brainstorm an alternative strategy, Cuddles' foot betrayed him, skidding on the loose gravel, and tumbled over the edge, towards the rocks below.

Bones exchanged a resigned glance with Be-Be and grumbled, "Looks like we're jumping after all."

And with that, they leapt into the unknown, their faith the only parachute they had.

Chapter Twenty-One

As the doors of an elevator slid open, Be-Be, Bones, and Cuddles stepped out, their expressions a mixture of shock and triumph. Against all odds, their gambit had paid off - they had arrived in Hell's reception area with all their intended cargo intact.

Sat behind the reception desk, Ivan the Terrible was equally stunned by their sudden reappearance. "Err, hi," he said awkwardly.

He picked up the phone and explained, "Bad Bitch wanted me to notify her immediately if you ever came back."

Be-Be, the master of manipulation, locked eyes with him and declared confidently, "You're mistaken. She told us to proceed without interruption and specifically mentioned that you shouldn't alert her of our presence."

"Oh, okay," he responded, his thoughts now clouded by her persuasive powers.

Be-Be felt a surge of relief wash over her. Since failing to breach Bad Bitch's mental defences a few months back, she had begun to question her abilities.

Bones's hand gripped the cold metal handle of the exit door, a sense of dread creeping over him. Casting a glance at his friends, he murmured, "I dread to think what's on the other side." With a steadying breath, he pushed the door open, unveiling a long concrete path that stretched for miles ahead, guiding them toward a foreboding and dark tower block.

An intense wave of heat washed over them, emanating from the vast expanse of seething molten lava that bordered the path on either side. Within the fiery depths writhed tormented souls enduring eternal suffering.

With weary determination, the trio embarked on their march down the desolate pathway, as the anguished wails of the damned reverberated around them. The weight of despair filled the air, each cry for mercy piercing their hearts as they trudged forward.

Motivated by empathy, Be-Be utilised her mind skills to rid numerous troubled individuals of their pain - as many as she could. The heartbroken woman looked out at the vast sea of suffering souls, and wished that she could help every one of them, but knew that it was an impossible task- for now.

As they approached the looming tower block, Be-Be's mental prowess came to their aid yet again, clearing their path by bending the will of every entity - be it a person, demon, or feral beast - that sought to stop them.

It finally fell to Bones to kick open the door to the main office, where they caught Bad Bitch and Oliver off guard, with the machine in the process of giving the woman a foot massage.

Taken aback by their sudden entrance, Bad Bitch was momentarily speechless, before finally commanding, "Oliver... *kill them*!"

Acting swiftly, Be-Be triggered the device, halting the android in its speedy tracks.

Bad Bitch appeared bewildered by their feat, her confusion deepening as she beheld the trio each aiming their water guns in her direction.

With a mischievous grin, Be-Be teased, "Squirt-prise, bitch!"

Cuddles shot his friend a disapproving look. "What was that?"

Embarrassed, she explained, "It was like... surprise! But... squirt-prise! Because of the water guns."

"Ah, I see. Well, yeah, I guess that works."

Bones interjected, "Perhaps we should just shoot her."

They all squeezed the triggers firmly, drenching the woman, who, to Be-Be's surprise, did *not* sizzle or melt as she had imagined. Instead, Bad Bitch appeared more irritated than anything, soaked to the bone.

"What the fuck are you doing?" the soaking woman shouted in frustration.

Be-Be sheepishly explained, "I thought perhaps water might be your kryptonite. Like, maybe, it might kill you."

"*No!*" Bad Bitch bellowed. "Who the fuck gets killed by water?"

"Kyle Poe," Cuddles interjected. "He drowned. Just saying."

"Well, I'm clearly not dead. But I am freezing and pissed off," Bad Bitch grumbled before raising her hand as though weaving a spell. "Be gone," she commanded with a flick of her wrist.

Nothing happened.

She tried again, "Be gone."

Just as before... nothing.

"Is something supposed to be happening?" Cuddles muttered.

It was then that Be-Be sensed her initial intuition about the water might have had merit. Bad Bitch wasn't dead, but she was affected nonetheless.

Approaching her foe, the once-deposed queen of the underworld sought to reclaim her dominion. She peered into Bad Bitch's eyes and commanded, "You *will* restore my reign over Hell."

Bad Bitch nodded compliantly, "You'll have your reign over Hell."

Be-Be had never been so grateful to have this talent. With a smirk, she continued, "You *will* return my infernal powers to me."

"Your infernal powers will be returned."

"And you *will* vacate these premises, *never* to return."

"I will vacate these premises and never return," she declared, poised to leave the room before suddenly dropping her facade.

"You *fools*!" she exclaimed. "Did you *truly* believe that would work? Just to clarify, *no*, water does not kill me, nor does it weaken me. It's just fucking *water*!"

Bones cast a glance at Be-Be and sighed, "I hate to say I told you so, but I did."

Swiftly, he retrieved a real gun concealed beneath his clothing and fired six bullets at Bad Bitch, who crumpled to the ground, lifeless.

"Apologies," Bones muttered awkwardly to Be-Be, "I didn't want to undermine you by bringing along something more lethal than frickin' *water*, but I'm kind of glad I did."

"Agreed," she chuckled.

They averted their eyes away from the deceased woman and to the office window, peering out at the desolate landscape below.

Be-Be announced, "Time to whip this place back into shape, with one small tweak."

Cuddles enquired, "Which is?"

"I'm thinking we bring in a new face to the management team."

As the underworld slowly returned to its prior state, Karina Reed was poised in the studio's makeup chair, prepping for her debut on the new show, 'Karina's Court Room'.

The makeup artist remarked, "So, assistant manager now, huh? Congrats."

"Thank you. And apparently it shouldn't interfere with the television work too much."

"That's good to hear because I can't wait to see this new gig of yours."

Casting a concerned glance at Reed's raw, blistered skin - a souvenir from her stint in the fiery pits - the artist pondered, "How the fuck am I supposed to fix this?"

She applied a dab of foundation to Reed's cheeks, which did absolutely nothing to conceal the damage, yet reassured her with a fib, "There, *much* better," before muttering to herself, "You definitely don't look like Freddy Krueger cosplay."

With an optimistic grin, the celebrity declared "Then it's time to make some television magic."

Nostalgia filled the air as Be-Be, Cuddles, and Bones settled back into their familiar spots within the studio.

A roar of applause shook the room as Reed skipped onto the stage. "Welcome to Karina's Court Room," she announced with fervour. "A show where two enemies will lay bare their grievances, and you, the viewers, vote which one will be devoured by wild beasts."

The host shared a fleeting smile with her companions, each looking utterly content. They were home. This is where they belonged.

Reed looked back into a camera and concluded, "Our first guests are a pair of mismatched housemates. Hitler insists that Bert, a 12-foot demon, needs to tone down his aggression, while Bert says that Hitler needs to simply stop being a little bitch. Let's welcome them to the stage!"

The End

Acknowledgements

I want to take the chance to really thank the unrelenting creatives I've had the privilege of knowing throughout my life. In a world quick to judge and label those who express themselves as attention-seeking or narcissistic, I genuinely see something different. I see a therapeutic outlet, someone getting joy from sharing something they're proud of for anyone who cares, and people just simply doing what they love.

It's all too easy to criticise and discourage. My friend Tom, who's all about making people laugh with his comedy skits, once got this comment that pretty much told him to give it up as he wasn't funny. That didn't sit right with me. I had to speak up because humour is subjective, right? What leaves one person stone-faced could have another rolling on the floor laughing. And it really bothers me to think about how many people have hung up their dreams due to the words of others.

To all of you who keep putting yourselves out there despite the likeliness of negativity, I can't help but admire you. You keep me motivated to keep exploring my own creative journey. So, don't stop doing your thing; you're killing it! And sure, this might come across as cheesy, and I fear rather preachy, but it's all genuine.

Finally, I'd like to give a special mention to the very first creative in my life - my sister, Sarah. Growing up around her and her poetry definitely sparked something in me.

Q&A

There are some real twisted scenes in this book. Are you a psychopath?
Next question.

This sequel followed a different formula from the original, which featured four short stories that tied together. What was the thought process behind that decision?

I took a slightly different path with the sequel because I wanted to tell a story that I felt couldn't be squeezed into a short burst. However, I intended for each act (the camping trip, Ivy Village and the worldwide massacre) to stand on their own much like short stories, whilst still being part of the one main narrative. And with the cutting back and forth between Earth and Hell, I'm hoping it still gave off the same vibes as the first book.

Throughout both books, you've told stories that have focused around a hypnotic ringmaster of a circus, superhero/supervillain, spoilt narcissist, social media sociopath and the world's first artificially intelligent President. Do you have a favourite?

The superhero story and Oliver, the AI president, hold a special place in my heart. They pushed me to think outside the box - how to blend the extraordinary with a touch of reality. Like when Night Protector botched his first mission because he didn't have a clue where to go - that's exactly what I imagine would happen in real life. And the idea of AI winning hearts and votes? Well, it makes sense when you think about how it would know the exact right thing to say to the right people – being able to charm the hell out of anyone! It was a lot of fun trying to ground these larger-than-life characters

I remember a review where someone pointed out how Night Protector felt too out of place at first, but before long, it felt like he was always meant to be there. That's exactly what I was aiming for - to weave the extraordinary into the fabric of the story so it felt completely natural.

How do you process and deal with negative book reviews?

The tears usually come when I'm close to finishing the first bottle of wine. By the time I'm halfway through the second bottle of wine, I start doubting my writing abilities and shouting in the mirror how I've failed and will never amount to anything. The next day, I regret deleting everything I've ever written. I am, of course, kidding… I drink Whisky.

What is the most difficult part of your writing process?

I do sometimes find it hard to motivate myself to start writing. It helps when I go into it thinking, "I'll just do a page," because chances are, once I've started, I'll continue. If not, that's okay too – I'm a page further into the story than I'd have been if I'd done nothing.

Which of the characters do you relate to the most and why?

Definitely Aiden in 7 1/2 Reasons Why I Hate This World. I'm very socially awkward and whilst I don't actually hate this world, I do get frustrated by a lot of things about society.

Throughout the story, the character goes off on many rants, one of these being;

"This is the first reason why I hate this world. Whether it be through society's expectations, science or whatever other potential facet - we're constantly being told how we should be thinking, feeling and living our lives. We're supposed to happily live in the box we've been placed in and should we dare to try and break the seal, so as to venture out of it, we're looked at and relabelled as weirdo's. I'm told what sauce I should be having with certain meats; I'm supposed to hold a conversation about football because I'm male. As a kid, I was encouraged to question my surroundings by teachers and other authoritative figures, but only up until a certain age - at which point I'm supposed to accept what I'm told by society, or be branded a conspiracy nut. I also played with toys as a child because it's a natural instinct to do so... but again, at a certain age we're supposed to cut that shit out too. The more we're told how to think, the less we actually think for ourselves, until eventually, we forget how to."

After reading the book, a friend of mine commented, "I can totally see you saying something like that in real life." Yes, I must be such a joy to be around! *makes mental note to be less annoying

What is the next book about?

I don't want to give too much away just yet, but it will focus on Virtual Reality in a way that is hopefully different to anything else out there. If you enjoyed the technology themes of this book, hopefully you'll enjoy the next one too. I'm really going to let my imagination run wild with it.

Any final words?

I'd like to thank everyone for reading this book. Sincerely, whether you loved it or hated it, it means the world that you took a chance on me and gave it a go.

A Christmas Coral (Chapter One)

After writing the first Devil's Replacement book, I began working on my third story; A Christmas Coral.

It's set in the enchanting Werrington Village, where a sinister shadow falls upon its idyllic façade. Meet Coral Bleek, a malevolent force that delights in the anguish she inflicts upon unsuspecting locals.

Aiden, a talented film student, finds his world shattered when Coral manipulates her daughter into ending her relationship with him. Determined to win her back, Aiden and his film-loving comrades find inspiration while watching the timeless classic, 'A Christmas Carol.' A daring idea takes hold: staging their own rendition of the beloved tale, with hopes of transforming Coral into a kinder and more compassionate soul.

In this uproarious farce, chaos takes the reins, and hilarity ensues as everything veers delightfully off course. From hilarious mishaps to unexpected twists, Aiden and his friends find themselves propelled into a whirlwind of absurdity. Will their madcap mission succeed in softening Coral's heart? Join them on this uproarious journey where love, laughter, and sheer mayhem collide in the most unexpected ways!

To help you decide whether this book is for you, here's the **first chapter**…

If I were to hazard a guess, I believe we must have broken around a dozen laws on Christmas Eve.

To my knowledge, everything I'm about to tell you is true. Much of it I heard from others, while certain parts I personally witnessed myself – like the disturbing incident at Jane's infamous party. I may actually need counselling just to get that image out of my head.

This is the story of Coral Bleek. The bitter old woman exuded an eerie aura, evoking fear in anyone brave enough to come near her as she paraded around Werrington Village, often in her beige cardigan with matching Louis Vuitton bag. Her stooped and skeletal figure was reminiscent of the formidable school principal we all dreaded in our childhood days. Wispy, silver locks clung to her scalp like delicate cobwebs, framing a face etched with deep lines from years of scowling.

To put it bluntly, Coral is a truly awful person. You may think that I'm simply being an overdramatic nineteen-year-old by saying so. Therefore, please allow me to provide you with some examples.

Firstly, just a few months ago, Coral called law enforcement officers to put an abrupt end to a business trading unlawfully near her home - this being due to their lack of appropriate paperwork. She watched on from her kitchen window with glee as the company's Chief Executive Officer broke down into tears, upon having their operation abruptly shut down. This crying was an understandable reaction given that it must have been a truly terrifying ordeal for the eight-year-old girl, who had simply been trying to sell lemonade.

Rumour has it, that this run in with the police changed the poor child from that moment on - resulting in an unhealthy relationship towards authority. She's since been seen eating pick and mix sweets out of the bag before weighing them at the register and she'll apparently purposely colour outside of the lines to, in her own words, feel alive.

Coral also once went door to door, demanding a stool sample from every dog in the neighbourhood. This was so she could begin her investigation into which canine had been crapping in her garden that day - with the mess being left, much to Coral's disgust. Naturally, no dog owner complied to this ludicrous request, but that didn't stop the tyrant hunting down the culprit.

After an all-night stakeout sat in her car, she'd never been so pleased to witness a pups' mess not being collected. A few tests gave the conclusive evidence of a match.

I can only imagine the look on this dog owners' face whilst unwrapping a mysterious gift box which contained... returned goods, alongside photographic evidence.

To say Coral is a frequent user on our village Facebook group would be an understatement. One recent post of hers went into great detail as to how she felt that a neighbours ten-foot inflatable snowman was too tacky and reflected badly on the area. A further three messages focusing around this matter were posted before a hooded assailant mercilessly stabbed Frosty multiple times during the night. It was difficult to believe that this was mere coincidence. The very next morning, Coral nonchalantly strolled past the crime scene, clutching a crushed ice fruit drink. Who consumes a slushy at

8am? Nobody! It was a clear message from her, unmistakably conveying, "Do not fuck with me."

The sociopath even directed an online post towards my own family once. She felt the need to publicly explain to my Mum that either my sister, Tracey, was having loud sex in her bedroom or being brutally attacked - suggesting that either way, she should perhaps go and put an end to it.

Coral also has one of the most pretentious houses I've ever seen. Her six bedroom mansion is filled to the brim with furniture covered in plastic. The reason for this is that the plastic apparently protects the fabric beneath, ensuring the furniture's everlasting beauty. You know what doesn't look beautiful? Furniture that is covered in frickin' plastic! The irony.

Within this abode, Coral had found it imperative to expand her wine cellar, dedicating a whole section to an utterly absurd assortment of wines exclusively for her feline companion. Believe it or not, this is very much a real thing. Since the discovery of this product, Coral was able to say that she technically never drank alone.

The woman even has gold plated toilet seats in each of her four bathrooms - which do not feel pleasant against bare ass cheeks. How do I know this? Well, I spent twenty minutes sat upon one of those toilets. The reason being is that frustratingly, Coral also happens to be the mother of my girlfriend, Donna.

The old saying goes; if you want to know what your girlfriend is going to look like in the future, just take a gander at the mother. I simply couldn't see that happening on this occasion though. With Donna's bouncy luscious golden hair that fell down to the waist, her cover model looks, and an hourglass figure that made heads swivel like owls – I found it hard to believe that she could ever end up looking *anything* like her Mum.

I vividly recall the moment my heart sank as my partner informed me about Coral's desire to host my family for dinner. She explained, "Mum is in two minds as to whether she wants to invite you all to dine with us on Christmas Day, so she wants to do a trial run a few weeks in advance."

"Like an audition?" I questioned, utterly bewildered.

"Essentially, yes."

"...Okay."

When the night finally came, things seemed surprisingly okay at first. My Mum and Tracey were on their best behaviour - being uncharacteristically courteous. Heck, even Uncle Dave was acting appropriately. That almost wasn't the case, of course. Prior to leaving our house, I had to practically beg him to put on a pair of trousers as opposed to his joggers with the hole in the crotch area. "Rich people don't appreciate comfort?" he queried. My counter-argument being that they don't appreciate a bollock popping out every now and then.

We all sat around a grand dining room table tucking into our sausage and mash. Even this humble British classic couldn't escape Coral's unyielding pretentiousness. Every bite felt like a pompous culinary experience, with artisanal sausages infused with rare spices, served on a bed of whipped potatoes infused with truffle oil. Let's not forget the garnish of microgreens, delicately arranged like some arty masterpiece. It was as if we were dining in a Michelin-starred restaurant, rather than someone's home.

I had been conveniently sat opposite the largest canvas I'd ever laid eyes on. It just so happened to portray a romantic picture of my girlfriend and, I assume, her ex-boyfriend - with the handsome fella seemingly making direct eye contact with me. My overactive imagination pictured him asking me the question, "Have you and Donna ever looked this happy? No, I didn't think so."

Beneath this enormous artwork sat Coral's husband, Colin. He appeared exhausted, with a vacant expression in his eyes, as if his mind was somewhere else entirely. I had my suspicions that this was perhaps his way of coping with the marriage. He initiated small talk by asking my family, "Have you made any holiday plans for next year?"

Mum explained, "We'll probably end up going to Happys again."

"Happys?" Coral asked. "Never heard of it."

"It's a caravan park we often visit."

"Like *gypsies*?" Coral gasped.

"Not exactly," Mum replied, quite taken aback by the offensive question. "Or maybe we'll just pitch a tent somewhere."

"Like the *homeless*?"

"I wouldn't put it that way, no," Mum said in an agitated tone. "Are you going anywhere yourselves?"

"We'll be jetting off to the French Riviera. Our villa is nestled up in the hills of St. Tropez and offers breathtaking panoramic views of the Mediterranean.

Uncle Dave enquired, "Any Bingo bars up there?"

"I... wouldn't have thought so, no."

"Karaoke?"

"...No."

"Titty bar?"

"No!"

"Not for me," Uncle Dave concluded.

"Well, I think it sounds lovely," Mum uttered awkwardly, feeling rather embarrassed about our plans compared to theirs.

In all honesty, I felt embarrassed too. I had never felt so poor before now. "I think I'll probably skip Happys next year," I explained, perhaps fuelled by the embarrassment. "I'm getting a bit too old for family holidays. Maybe I'll jet off somewhere too."

I think I may have subconsciously thrown in that last line in an attempt to impress Coral. I kind of hated myself a little for doing so.

Mum gave me a knowing look, seeing right through my bullshit. She sighed, "You know, there's a good chance that Santa has already booked next year's tickets to Happys. Sorry."

Naturally, I felt awful about this revelation.

Clearing her throat, Mum picked up her handbag and continued, "Speaking of gifts.... Coral, we have a little something for your wine cellar."

"That's very kind of you, Jill."

Coral's enthusiasm quickly dwindled upon seeing the bottle. She reluctantly took it like it were an infected phallus.

Colin expressed his delight, saying, "How lovely. What year is written on the bottle dear?"

"It's hard to say," his wife croaked back whilst examining the beverage. "Literally, the one and only thing printed on the bottle is the word 'Red'."

"Well, we're very *grapeful* for it," he humorously responded, eliciting mostly forced chuckles from those gathered around the table.

Uncle Dave, on the other hand, genuinely burst into laughter as if it were the most hilarious play on words that he had ever heard. "Comedy gold," he said enthusiastically.

"Don't encourage him," Coral sneered whilst shaking her head disapprovingly. "Stop trying to show off, Colin. You're *not* funny."

The poor guy sat there with his head down, defeated, like a wounded puppy.

Once his laughter died down, Uncle Dave chimed in, "If you guys enjoy the wine, my girlfriend can get this stuff for fifty pence per bottle. If anyone asks, they accidentally fell off the back of a lorry."

With no effort to hide her look of disgust, Coral responded, "I think I'd rather pay the extra fifty pence and purchase them legally."

"Fair enough," he replied awkwardly. "If you change your mind, let me know."

Shifting the tone, Tracey asked my girlfriend, "You both met in college, right?"

"We did," she replied. "Embarrassingly, he passed my car with me crying my eyes out inside it - traumatised from a recent breakup."

"A breakup with the guy on the canvas?"

"Yup," Donna confirmed. "Aiden tapped on my window and was super sweet and caring towards me. The rest is history."

Concerned that these words made me sound like a creep preying on someone at their most vulnerable, I was quick to clarify, "We were just friends for *months* after that, before anything actually happened."

"And *what* has happened?" Coral snapped.

I nervously confirmed, "Us becoming boyfriend and girlfriend."

Uncle Dave threw me a smile and a look that appeared to say, "It's okay, I'll handle this."

I desperately shook my head to deter him, but typically, he didn't pick up on the social cue.

"Don't worry, Coral... I don't think they're having sex," he reassured. "He wanks *way* too much for someone that's having sex."

At this point, I was under no doubt that we'd failed the "audition" for that Christmas Day invite.

"Red card," I screamed, truly mortified.

My Uncle has a knack for blurting out the absolute worst stuff at the most inconvenient moments. Eventually, the family came up with a brilliant plan to tame his tongue: the football penalty system. Whenever he begins his infamous inappropriate ramblings, we'll unleash the mighty cry of, "Yellow card!" That is his official warning. Should he escalate his shenanigans, out comes the metaphorical "Red card!" When that crimson card is thrust upon him, he's got two choices: shut his trap on the spot or scram, making a hasty exit from the area.

Uncle Dave fulfilled his obligation to cease verbal communication but was still able to up the level of awkwardness. We all sat there, utterly horrified, as we witnessed him nervously thrusting his sausage into the mashed potatoes, creating a bizarre spectacle that resembled a rather unconventional form of intimacy.

It was all too much for me to bear. "I'm just going to nip to the toilet," I panicked before making my escape.

I genuinely never intended for my refuge in the bathroom to stretch into an epic twenty-minute confinement. It's just that the mere thought of returning to that table filled me with terror, rendering me motionless.

During this extended stay, I found myself captivated by a festive scene sat on the windowsill. Someone had skilfully crocheted the classic Christmas nativity, complete with baby Jesus, a donkey, and the three wise men, among others. It was quite the impressive sight.

To further pass the time, I made the impulsive decision to learn how to juggle - using bath bombs as my juggling props. Unfortunately, I peaked at a measly two.

I also found myself engrossed in videos on my phone featuring clueless teenagers experimenting with a newfangled drug that had taken the nation by storm. This illegal, magical concoction known as 'Extro-spurt' had the power to transform even the most introverted individuals into paragons of confidence. As was the way in this modern world, the hilarious results were often captured on film for everyone's entertainment.

In one particular recording, a group of friends had been awkwardly going door to door, muttering Carol songs in hopes of pocketing a few extra quid. One home owner would later regret saying, "I'm just having dinner. Come back later." Under the influence of a few 'Extro-spurts' at around 2 a.m., their guilt-ridden minds were tortured by the fact that they never did return to that home. They had lied! The teens quickly convinced themselves that it was their moral duty to return and surprise the woman in her bedroom, making the experience as hassle free for her as possible. They woke the stranger to a significantly more enthusiastic rendition of 'O Little Town of Bethlehem.' Needless to say, the terrified victim did not appreciate the breaking and entering. Nor did the police, who had to forcibly drag the friends away during their final song, 'Silent Night'.

My video viewing pleasure came to an abrupt end with a sudden knock at the bathroom door.

Startled, I swiftly paused the clip I was half way through watching.

Donna timidly asked, "Are you alright, Aiden?"

"Yeah, yeah, I'm fine," I stammered, feeling a wave of embarrassment wash over me as I realised just how long I had been holed up in there.

"Dad was wondering if you've run out of toilet paper or something."

A deep shade of red flooded my face as the embarrassment reached new heights. "Um, no, everything's fine," I replied. "Thanks for checking, though."

"Okay... well... hopefully we'll see you downstairs shortly."

With my girlfriend gone, I looked around the room and a horrible realisation hit me. I, in fact, *did* need toilet roll. But I had surely missed the one opportunity to be given some without it being *too* awkward. I therefore needed to improvise.

Scanning my surroundings, I looked for something suitable to wipe with - a random sock, a sanitary pad, scrap paper - absolutely anything! Desperation even had me rummaging through the bathroom bin but to no avail.

It quickly dawned on me what I needed to do. "I'm so sorry, baby Jesus," I sighed whilst reaching for the crocheted son of God.

Mere inches away from my ass, I stopped. I was in no way a religious person, but this just felt wrong. I ultimately swapped the child for the donkey and did the business before plunging the evidence deep into the bottom of the bin - terrified that the soiled creature could cause a flood if flushed down the toilet.

I'm almost certain that a transparent look of guilt was planted across my face whilst returning to the dining room table. I fumblingly rejoined the family and the silence was deafening.

"Everything okay?" I asked nervously.

There were a few unconvincing nods across the table.

I continued, "What have I missed?"

Coral explained, "I was just telling your family about Donna's remarkable achievement of receiving straight A-plus grades last year."

Sheepishly, Donna added, "One of them was just an A. Not an A-plus."

Her mother was quick to confirm, "Initially, yes. But then you retook the exam and fixed the problem."

I couldn't quite believe what I was hearing.

Uncle Dave chimed in, "And that led me to explain how *your* grades spelt the word 'Fudge'... which was spooky because your dead dad loved eating Fudge. It was like he was with you that day."

Don't worry, I was used to these thoughtless comments.

Coral interjected, her voice carrying a hint of concern. "I proceeded to share my observation about Donna's ex-fiancé, a prosperous lawyer. It struck her father and I as peculiar that after their breakup, she'd swiftly move on to someone so... contrasting."

I noticed my mother's firm grip on her cutlery, sensing the tension in the air. What unfolded next was an uncomfortable showdown between the two mothers, and mine took the first shot. "In that moment," she growled, "I made it clear that while your wallet may not overflow with riches, your heart overflows with boundless love."

"I then explained how boundless love does not pay the bills."

"To which I stressed that, at your age, you shouldn't be worrying about how to pay the bills. You're still trying to work out who you are."

"And I pointed out that Donna knows exactly who she is already... an apprentice at one of the finest law firms in the country."

"I then asked if I could have Tracey's sausage," Uncle Dave declared. "If she wasn't planning on eating it."

Coral concluded the thorough details by saying, "My husband mentioned that you had been in the bathroom for quite a while and might need some assistance, like toilet paper. And now that you're fully updated, perhaps it's time to call it a night. My husband heads off to work at 9, which also happens to be my bed time. But before that, we like to watch our favourite television show, which has already started.

We were all *more* than happy to make our escape. With zero hesitation, the family began to gather our belongings. Whilst doing so, Uncle Dave asked, "Do you always work nights, Colin?"

"Yes, unfortunately. I'm just waiting for retirement... or death - whichever comes first," he replied with a half-joking tone. "My body is practically broken but thanks to some damn fine painkillers, I'm able to persist."

"Yes, we can still squeeze a few more paychecks out of you," Coral added, sounding even less like a joke.

Uncle Dave probed further, "Will you be working over Christmas?"

"I'll be working Christmas Eve. Not Christmas Day, but I'll probably sleep through most of it."

As we rose from our seats, the questioning wasn't quite finished. "What show are you watching?" Uncle Dave persisted.

"Karina Reed Believes," Coral snapped impatiently, glancing at her watch.

"Jill and I *love* that show," Uncle Dave replied, much to our dismay.

We all knew the polite response to this, but whether an invitation to join them would actually be given was another matter.

Colin hesitated for a moment before muttering, "Well... you're all welcome to stay and watch it with us, if you'd like?"

Coral shot him a glare, her eyes filled with daggers. It mirrored the same look we exchanged with Uncle Dave when he responded, "We'd *love* to."

I knew exactly what my family were thinking in that moment. "Red card!"

Printed in Great Britain
by Amazon